THE *Family* FIRM

The Santini Family #1

S.L. Sinclair

Partners in Crime Book Services

ISBN: 979-8-9988203-0-4

Writing on the dark side.

Table of Contents

Content Warning

<u>Please skip this page if you do not want a warning.</u>

This book is meant for readers above the age of 18 due to sexual content, dubious consent, non-consent, kidnapping, physical abuse, torture, murder, and a slight instance of drug use.
It also includes MM content and incest.
Read at your own discretion.

Also by S.L. Sinclair

Beyond Her Duties (MF)

The Family Firm (RH)

The Family Secret (RH)

The Family Fortune (RH)

Wife For Hire (MF)

Call Me Danger (RH)

Don't Get Me Twisted (RH)

Please Love Me (MMMM)

Unbiased (RH)

Acts of Contrition (MF)

Her Secret Master (MF)

The Vampire Mistress (FF)

Perfect Disaster (MF)

Lie To Me (MM)

Playlist

"Man Made Machine" by MOTOR feat. Martin L. Gore

"Alone I Break" by KoRn

"Cloud Nine" by Evanescence

"Deeper and Deeper" by Dave Gahan

"Take Me Back Home" by Soulsavers

"I'll Follow You" by Shinedown

"Wicked Game" by Chris Issac (Stone Sour's cover)

"Too Drunk…" by Buckcherry

"Home Grown" by OTEP

"The Nameless" by Slipknot

"Lick Me" by JDevil

"Summertime" by My Chemical Romance

"Cut Up Angels" by The Used

"XO" by Fall Out Boy

Chapter One

Sasha

"THAT IS IT. You're never going out at night without at least two other people!" Mom scolds as we sit down to watch the evening news after my younger siblings are asleep.

I glance over at her. "I don't go out alone," I insist. "Only losers do that."

The TV headline is lurid: *"Serial Abuser Loose in City"*. It's meant to get people scared, and it is doing its job. Mom's plenty scared, and while I realistically know the sexual assault statistics, I doubt the news' credibility.

"Two girls were taken from the same popular section of downtown, taken to a house, and let go. Neither can give a location of the house, and the descriptions of the abductors are different. I doubt it's the same guy. One guy probably saw the original report and did a copycat. And both will give up now that these girls are on the news," I say logically.

Not that I'm one of those cuckoos who yell "FAKE NEWS" whenever there's something on TV I disagree with. I'm a law school hopeful once I get past this summer and head over to the biggest college in the state. So I pride myself on my logic and problem-solving. Any prosecutor would be in deep shit to try a case based on the evidence the news is broadcasting to the entire county.

"This being two random people and not one doesn't make me feel any better," she comments, sipping her tea.

I smile at her and pat her hand. "Don't worry, Mom. Besides, these girls were drunk. I'm not old enough to drink. So that kinda rules me out as these pervs' type. *But*," I emphasize the word as I see her about to protest, "the next time my friends and I go out, I promise to call you or Daddy to pick me up. I won't Uber or take the bus."

Mom huffs, either because she can't argue with my logic or because I mentioned Daddy. They have a fairly friendly divorce and co-parent my younger siblings well, but an ex is an ex, and she hasn't quite gotten over the split.

"All right. Thank you, honey."

I tilt my head back in relief and sip my steaming mug of hot cocoa. I want to comment on how Daddy's was always better, even from the packet, but refrain. No need to rub salt in the wound.

Even though the split was about eighty percent Mom's fault.

"Speaking of Gene..."

Guess it is Mom's turn to rub salt in her own wound.

"Yeah?"

"Tony wants to have his annual pool party for the 4th of July this year. We're all invited."

I smile; I'm not too big on swimming, but I've always enjoyed hanging out at Uncle Tony's place. Frankly, everybody does. He's the ultimate bachelor, dates a ton of gorgeous women, and his house is basically a funhouse. There's a game room, another "man cave" where he and I would watch baseball with my little brother, a sauna, and the backyard has a mini golf course and a huge in-ground pool. His grill is nearly restaurant-worthy, and he's a great cook.

Plus, he usually takes the entertainment side of the family's law firm, so you can find famous people just milling about. It's awesome.

"He said you can invite friends," Mom continues. "But he said Trevor is not allowed."

"Good, I don't want him around," I assure her. "That last break up was for real. I'm done with immature assholes who can't communicate."

"We'll all feel better when you go more than a month without him," Mom replies, getting out her phone to presumably text Uncle Tony that I will be sans boyfriend.

"I went six weeks in freshman year," I say, knowing full well that's only going to irritate her. The look she gives me makes me laugh. "Okay, I know, I've been stupid. But I swear, this breakup is for real. I don't need my last few months of senior year ruined by him and his ego that's way bigger than his dick."

Mom holds her hand up and pretends to vomit. "TMI! TMI!" she cries, using the acronym.

I smile and stand up, giving her a kiss on the cheek. My mom and I don't always see eye to eye. In fact, I think we've not spoken more than we have spoken due to our arguments. So this is a nice change. It has been worse in the past two years without Daddy to intervene. I'm pretty pleased with how the night has gone.

I rinse my mug and head upstairs to bed. It's a Friday, and while I kinda want to skip, I have to drive my siblings to school, so I figure I'll go, too.

Speaking of...

"Sasha?"

I turn to see my youngest sibling, Caleb, peeking at me from his bedroom door.

"What are you doing?" I whisper. "If Mom catches you up at eleven, she'll flip her shit, kid."

He beckons me inside and I sigh and oblige, shutting his door behind me. He has his bedspread propped up with a ruler and a flashlight over what looks like a school project. The family tree. I had to do one, too, when I was his age, for Social Studies.

"I didn't finish, and it's due!" he says, hopping from one foot to the other. "I didn't know how to add you."

I give him a smile and motion towards his bed. "All right, go sit. I'll show you. I had to add you and Maggie the same way." I lean down and point next to our mom. "Put a line with a slash in it from Mom to her ex. You don't need to name him."

I don't know his name anyway. I'm not sure Mom does, either.

"Okay, now draw a line down the middle of them with my name. That shows I'm your half sister," I explain.

He does so and sighs like he ran a marathon. "Oh man, thanks! This is my last assignment for Social Studies this year, and Mr. Thompson is a bastard."

I giggle at his cursing. He definitely didn't come from a virtuous family. I'm waiting for the day he calls his principal a cunt or something and gets suspended.

I give him a kiss on the top of his head and go to leave, but he calls me back.

"I hate it that Maggie and I get to see Dad and you don't."

I smile a little. "I text him and stuff. This is your time with him, not mine. And we'll all hang out this summer at Uncle Tony's, just like old times."

He perks up at that. "Promise?"

I nod. "Cross my heart."

I know adults usually lie to kids, but I refuse to. I love my half-siblings, and I love my step family. Mom's family treats us like we don't exist because Mom got pregnant with me when she was eighteen and unmarried. Daddy's family is all I've known.

In my room, I glance at the pictures I keep on my dresser. One of them is Mom's wedding to Daddy. I was their flower girl at age five, and I looked so happy back then. And Mom and Daddy were together for eleven happy years.

Well, mostly happy.

I used to hear their arguments, but I never quite understood half of them because I was so little. Now I know better, and I kinda wish I didn't.

Nobody needs to know that their mom is a "frigid bitch".

I was close with Daddy and still am, but it's not the same without him living here. And because he offered to pay for my friends and I to go to Universal City for my eighteenth birthday, he even missed that big event in my life.

Sitting at my computer, I log into social media and decide to do one quick check of it all before I go to sleep.

I smirk as I spy a new picture Uncle Tony posted. He's got yet another girlfriend, this one a brunette who looks maybe twenty-five. The girl isn't tagged, and some of Uncle Tony's friends left amusing comments.

Daddy left one, too: *"I bet this one lasts three weeks."*

I comment under Daddy, *"You're on: I bet she won't last two."*

Uncle Tony gives us both a middle finger emoji and I dissolve into giggles, trying not to wake my sister. Her room and mine share a wall.

The messenger icon lights up with a red '1' and I open it right away, thinking it's Uncle Tony or maybe Daddy. Of course, my overzealousness backfires.

It's from Trevor, my now permanently ex-boyfriend.

"This isn't gonna last. You're going to come back to me one way or another. You always have, and you always will."

Chapter Two

Sasha

I CAN'T AVOID the news even while hanging out with my friends. Not that I have many. I'm not exactly sociable. But I somehow manage to hang onto the popular crowd by the skin of my teeth and the fact that my Daddy represents some of the biggest sports stars in the city at the family firm.

We're all seniors, all eighteen, but I swear these girls forget they're not twelve anymore, and the boys haven't aged since second grade.

Ah well, once summer comes, I never need to see them again.

"Are you scared?"

I jump from my thoughts as Tessa addresses me. "What?"

"Earth to Sasha. Are you scared to go out because of all this bullshit on the news?"

I shake my head. "No. Look, creeps are out there all the time. If I lived my life scared, I'd never live at all."

"And there's your yearbook quote," another friend, Abby, says with a laugh. "I like it."

"Anyway, my dad just invested in The Green Room," Tessa continues. "And we're all on the guest list."

Everyone sort of talks over each other, and my protests that it's not a good idea are completely drowned out. Eventually, I fall into the conversation and help come up with the lie we're using on our parents, because none of them are ever happy when Tessa's dad invites us to places we're not legally allowed to get into. He does it because we all look good — I know that because he said so once. But still, it's illegal. And especially my mom will kill me.

"And we really can stay at my place after," Tessa finishes, eyes shining like we're going to Paris or Rome and not some skeezy nightclub.

I sigh into my chocolate milk. As much as I want to go out, this weekend is going to be ridiculous … and not in a good way.

* * *

As predicted, Mom tries to talk me out of even going to a sleepover.

Finally, I snap. "Mom! I don't think some psycho is going to break into one of the most well-protected gated communities just to try and get to a houseful of girls. Calm down!"

She narrows her eyes at me and points a manicured index. "You might be eighteen, but you are still my daughter and will not talk to me like that!"

"I have to, or else you don't listen to a word I say," I retort, tossing a pair of pajamas into my tiny overnight bag. "I don't know what you're always so worried about: people get kidnapped and assaulted at everyday places. It's not exclusive to going out — which I am not, by the way. You let me walk to the drugstore by myself. I could get hit by a car for fuck's sake!"

I roll my eyes at her back as she turns and stalks out of my room. That means I won, because she can't come up with a response.

I finish packing and book a rideshare, because I don't want to have to struggle with parking in Tessa's semi-circle driveway. I know some of the guys will be driving, and they're liable to crash into my car.

Tessa's family's mansion is bigger than ours, taking up space they don't need. Daddy was adamant we not have more than what we could use, and I'm grateful. Our house is a home; Tessa's is a mausoleum.

The housekeeper lets me in and I go right up to Tessa's bedroom, which is as big as an apartment, and filled with our female friends getting ready. The stench of bad Victoria's Secret body sprays makes me gag. Why do rich girls insist on wearing this crap?

"Sash!" she cries, giving me a wobbly hug. They've been pregaming. "Get dressed! Let me do your makeup!"

"No offense, but you're more likely to poke my eyes out," I reply.

"Don't be such a stick in the mud," she comments, passing me a shot glass from the side table.

I take a sniff and smell something almost like anisette. Jagermeister. I down the shot, relishing the burn in my throat before I get dressed.

I put on a pink and lavender plaid pleated miniskirt and a sparkly pink top that makes my boobs look bigger than they are. The colors offset my olive skin, or so I read online somewhere.

I put on my makeup while my friends squeal and fuck around. Not that I don't like them — I do. But I'm not like them. I've never been into the stuff

they're into except fashion. We only
hang out because our parents hang out.
I'm happy to be included, but I'm not
going to miss them when I go to college
in the fall. I should add, I am not one of
those "I'm not like other girls"
misogynists. A lot of women are like me.
I just happen to not be like my friends.

The six of us pile into Abby's
BMW sedan. She drew the short straw
and is our designated driver. The guys
are all going to meet us there instead of
going to Tessa's.

When we pull into downtown and
find the club, there's a line down the
block; it mingles in with *other* clubs'
lines.

Abby whistles. "Tess, your dad
has made a goldmine. Even if we were
twenty-one, we'd never get in here
without you."

"Your gratitude feeds me," she replies with a giggle, which makes everyone else giggle.

She leads us to the front door and gives her name. "Have the gentlemen from my party arrived?"

"Yes, Miss Toole," the growly doorman says. "You ladies have fun." We all get a hand stamp as we pass him by.

I expected a dance club that plays the same beat over and over at slightly different tempos, but am pleasantly surprised that a remix of a popular rock song blares instead. Something I actually like.

The lights flash in time with the music in all the colors of the rainbow, then a white strobe goes off, and then back to the somehow dim brightness. Does that make sense?

You can see, but you can't *see*. The air conditioning is blasting, and the bodies are only pressed together if they want to be; there's room to move around and mingle as we please. There's a VIP section with a smaller dance floor and purple velvet couches and chairs. There's an air of mystery about the place I feel as though I should like. But I'm uneasy, and I don't know why.

Tessa shoves a glass of vodka tonic at me. "You're getting drunk," she announces.

"That is the plan," I agree, taking the glass and downing half. I need to pace myself after the Jager. And I will. Later.

"We also need to get you laid," she adds.

"I do not need to get laid," I counter, immediately downing the other half of my drink. "Trevor took over my life since freshman year. What I need is to be single."

Tessa nods as if that's exactly what she said. "I agree. I want you to have sex, not get a boyfriend. Big diff!"

I nod now, waving down the bartender for another drink. I don't want anything casual, either. As far as I'm concerned, my pussy has a 'temporarily closed' sign on it. But telling Tessa that is the equivalent of telling a Texan the South lost the Civil War.

After my second drink, I feel good enough to dance as MOTOR and Martin Gore's "Man Made Machine" starts blaring. I don't like dance music, but you can't hear anything by Martin and *not* want to move.

Tessa brings me a third drink, and she's already so many deep I can't keep count. But the liquor keeps flowing and the music plays and I'm lost in the beat and the vibe. I wind up dancing with a few different people, including Tessa, who gets a little handsy, but I don't mind. She's stuck up, but I'm not blind.

A few of the men try to get handsy, too, and the more I drink, the better a quickie in the club bathroom looks.

Trevor was as close to a sex fiend as a teenager could get, and his insatiable appetite meant I either had to keep up, or he'd make me keep up.

Learned that one the hard way.

But thanks to him, I realize I can't exactly close myself off for business. My body demands as much as he was giving me, and until I can safely hide sex toys in my bedroom, I need the real thing.

Someone starts dancing with me from behind, one hand groping a breast and the other on my hip. It feels good, but I think anything would at this point. The hand on my hip moves lower, up my skirt, fingers caressing my thigh. Then higher, over the crotch of my panties and I whine, trying to turn and see who the guy is at least. He holds fast, however, hooking a hand tightly in the thin lace and yanks. Some elastic snaps against me, and the feeling just makes my pussy throb harder. Fingers invade again, this time with nothing in between them and my wetness.

The song ends, and I hear a painfully familiar voice hiss in my ear, "I made you a slut, and you'll always be just that: my fucking slut."

I whirl around to face ... Trevor. My blond haired, blue eyed football player ex-boyfriend. *How* could Tessa invite him?

I feel so betrayed. I left him for a reason this time, a good fucking reason, and she had no business bringing him to this club.

He holds my panties with one hand and tries to pull me closer with the other, but somehow I scamper away like a scared rabbit and avoid his touch. And once I start to move, I can't stop. My last sight of him is his laughter as a friend high fives him and he waves my panties in the air like a prize.

I have to get out of here.

Now.

I stumble out of the bar, angry, frustrated, and horny on top of it.

How dare he touch me like that? Fucking prick.

As I walk, I see headlights behind me but don't think anything of it. It's a busy street. Then the lights slow down, and I instantly regret all my posturing and saying I wasn't scared.

Because alone, drunk, at past midnight on a Saturday, I'm scared. I'm also stupid. Goosebumps rise on my arms and the back of my neck. I can feel the driver's eyes on me. I cross my arms to feel as small as possible and pick up my pace.

Bad idea. At least, bad while drunk and wearing four-inch heels. The sidewalk is nearly empty — most people are at home or in the clubs down the street. I stumble, try to catch myself on the parking meter, but fall on my back, the wind knocked out of me.

"Miss, are you okay?" a man's voice calls. The car has stopped, parking in the empty spot by the traitorous parking meter.

I want to get away, *need* to get away, but my body won't move right.

"Sasha?"

How does the rapist know my name?

I look up in surprise as Uncle Tony's face looms above. Relief washes over me and my tense body relaxes.

Until I realize Trevor took my panties, and my legs are spread wide open in this miniskirt. And Uncle Tony is basically standing between them.

His eyes roam over me and he shakes his head. "C'mon, Sash. Let's get you standing." He walks to the side of me and grabs me by both arms, lifting me first into a sitting position and then to stand.

The sudden movements make me dizzy again, and I lean against him heavily. He reaches around me to lift me more, and one hand grabs a generous handful of breast. Shockwaves go down my body, and Uncle Tony doesn't say anything as he moves his hand to my waist, keeping me steady.

A small bit of me that's still sober scolds me for having any sort of reaction to that accidental touch, but I'm too drunk to bother to listen. Big green eyes stare at me, and I realize I've been staring at Uncle Tony's hands on me for too long.

"What the fuck did you drink?" he asks with a chuckle.

"Jager," I reply. "And vodka."

He arches his eyebrows and tightens his hold on me as he opens the passenger-side door. "All right. In you go, tesoro."

I feel my cheeks flame. He hasn't called me that in like five years. That means 'treasure'. I manage to get in the car without making a fool of myself again.

As Uncle Tony gets in the driver's seat, I'm still struggling with the seatbelt.

"Let me get that," he offers.

I move my arms to my sides as he leans over me to grab the seatbelt. His body is turned and his arm presses into my stomach, right under my breasts. I suck in a breath as my already turned on body betrays me even more, wanting him to keep pressing me down...

This is your fucking uncle, you pervy bitch, my brain screams.

Step-uncle, I internally argue with myself.

He's known you since you were five!

I shake my head and disperse my conscience. She's a lot of trouble if you ask me.

"There," he says, clicking it into place. "You too drunk to focus or lost in thought?" An eyebrow arches.

"Thinking," I reply. "Maybe I'm not drunk enough."

He chuckles as he pulls out of the parking spot and begins to drive. "Open the glove compartment."

I do as he asks, and find a few airplane bottles of alcohol in there.

"I keep those for when clients are driving me batshit," he explains. "Go on."

I arch my eyebrows at him. This isn't totally new. Daddy and Uncle Tony and Nonno all allowed us kids a little wine or brandy. It's just an Italian thing. But to offer me something while I'm already shitfaced? That's a whole new level of "cool uncle".

"Are you sure?" I ask, already reaching for a small bottle of Grey Goose.

"Why not? This may be the hangover that makes you swear off alcohol for life ... or at least until next weekend."

I laugh and drink half the little bottle in a swallow, relishing the smooth burn only good alcohol — not the cheap shit — can give.

"How'd you get into a club and get served anyway?" he wonders. "Doing something you shouldn't on your knees?"

"What? No! Tessa's dad owns it. We weren't carded or policed," I reply, but my mind lingers on what he insinuated. "And if I had done anything like that, I'd never tell."

"Not even me?" he asks, playfully pouting.

I don't answer and instead look out the window. We're leaving the city behind now and I put my head in my hands and groan.

"Mom's gonna kill me when she finds out I went and left without my friends."

"Hang on, sweetheart. I've got you. Where does she think you are?"

"Tessa's dad's house. He lives near you," I reply.

He reaches for his phone, which is docked on the dashboard, and calls my mother. "Hey, Gina. It's Tony. Sasha gave me a call, but I wanted to tell you anyway: her friend's party was a little over the top... She's perfectly fine. A little tipsy. I don't want to keep her in a car for too long, so I'm gonna have her sleep it off at my place. That all right with you? ... You bet. And don't worry, I will. Talk soon." He hung up and turned towards me. "Your mother wants me to remind you that underage drinking is a crime, and she will demand that my father not take you on as a client if you ever get busted."

I giggled. "That sounds like Mom. Thanks for that, Uncle Tony. You don't mind me sleeping over?"

He turns towards me for a second and a large, warm hand settles heavily on my thigh. "Of course not, tesoro. I have just the spot for you."

Chapter Three

Sasha

NCLE TONY'S HOUSE looks even more massive to my drunk, unfocused eyes. Two of me standing on top of each other could fit under the door frame. But the house is like Tony: broad, strong, and stunning to look at.

"So, tell me something," he asks as he helps me from the car. I stumble as I try to stand. That last vodka he gave me really hit me hard. "Do you usually go commando at these parties?"

My face must be a tomato by now. "Um, no. My stupid ex … well, it's a long story."

He tightens his hold on me to keep me upright as he opens the front door. "Still trying to get in your pants after you told him to fuck off?" he guesses.

I nod, and regret it as the movement makes the foyer spin.

"Well, I can't blame him," Uncle Tony admits. "You're gorgeous. I'd never let you go if I got my hands on you."

Wait, what? Did he just say that, or is the liquor messing with my hearing?

"Kick those heels off," he instructs as he also removes his shoes.

I do as he asks, only to once again stumble backwards, but luckily he catches me. Without my heels, I'm 5'3" to his 6'1", and the difference is noticeable to say the least. My head only comes up to his sternum, and my hand can't close around his wrist as I grab on to remain steady.

"Silly girl," he says, his voice a low rumble in his chest. I can feel it vibrate and I feel like I should cross my legs as it makes my core ache. "Come on. Up you get."

In one quick movement, he sweeps me into his arms, bridal-style. My miniskirt rises up and I can literally feel a breeze on my unmentionables. He turns and walks up the stairs as easily as if he were carrying a couple of pillows and not a fully grown human woman.

He leads me to one of the guest rooms, though this one is extremely sparsely furnished compared with the rest of his house. The bed wouldn't be out of place in a prison, and there's a small TV in front of it. He deposits me on the bed abruptly, unlike the delicate way he'd carried me.

My unbalanced, drunk self lands on my ass, but my legs are splayed, revealing my wet slit to the man I've called "uncle" since I was five years old.

He scoffs. "Aren't you a needy one? First you somehow let your ex take your panties, after that you spread your legs on the sidewalk, then you let me grope you, and now you're silently begging for it."

"What? No, all that … it was an accident," I say, trying to get my brain to think clearly, but I can't.

"Sure it was," he mocks, stepping between my legs. He reaches out and pulls at my sparkly pink tank top until it tears away, leaving my breasts bare. My nipples immediately harden in the air.

I cover up, but that makes me move too much on the bed so I move one arm to prop me up. I need to sit up, I need to get out. Whatever's gotten into him, somehow I feel like I made it worse.

This far down, I get a good eyeful of the growing bulge in his jeans. It doesn't look long, but it looks thick.

That could ruin me…

I shake my head to dispel that thought. It's wrong. It's knocking on the house next door to incest. But alcohol and common sense don't really go together, and heat rises in my cheeks as I keep staring, transfixed.

Uncle Tony chucks me under the chin so I have to look up into his face. "Tesoro, I know you want this. I know you need this. Why are you fighting?

Don't you think Uncle Tony knows what's best for you?"

I nod, his words and deep voice wrapping themselves around me like a blanket.

"Unzip my jeans. Show me what those pretty pink lips can do, sweet girl," he commands. He lets my chin go and moves back a step. Just enough room for me to run, to leave, before this gets even more out of hand.

His green eyes glance from me to the door then back to me, a triumphant smirk on his lips when he sees I'm not going anywhere.

A conversation from when I was sixteen comes to mind, between Tessa and I the last time I went to Uncle Tony's pool party, Trevor in tow.

"God, between your dad and your uncle, I'd be going straight to Hell if I was in your position," she said.

"What? Why?" I asked. Trevor had been arguing with me and my mind was preoccupied.

Tessa grinned. "Have you looked at them? They're sexy as fuck. Tony looks like a model. I'd happily be jailbait for him, and anything else he wanted."

I looked over at him, laughing with someone I didn't know, wet swim trunks clinging to everything that was important, and felt my face flush.

"See?" Tessa said. "You agree. That cock is soft and could break me. And I'd happily let it."

She mentions him even now. Once in a while she mentions Daddy, too. I try to tune her out. I mean, they're my family, right?

My rambling thoughts are halted as Uncle Tony's cock pops free of his jeans and underwear, already half hard with a reddening tip. My hand practically glides down it, ghosting over the thick ridges of veins and back up again. I duck my head, way too unsteady to get to and remain on my knees, and press a gentle kiss to its tip.

Uncle Tony hisses and I take that as a compliment as I open my mouth and suck the tip in, tasting salt and sweat and precum. His strong hand comes to the back of my head but doesn't try to maneuver me. He's just ... holding me there, moving with me as I dip my head to take him in further.

"Oh, good girl," he praises.

That goes right to my core and I moan a little around his cock, wanting to take him deeper if I can. Trevor was adamant about me being a good cocksucker, and at least I could thank him for one thing as I felt Uncle Tony's cock go past my throat, not activating my gag reflex.

I move back again and focus on sucking, on pleasing him.

Finally, he pulls me off of his cock and lifts me one-handed until I'm standing before him. Still holding me by the hair, he pulls me closer and kisses me on the mouth, something I didn't expect since his cock so recently vacated there.

I kiss back, trying to keep up as his tongue plunders my mouth in a wet, hungry, demanding manner. His other arm snakes around my now bare waist and presses my breasts to his silk dress shirt. It moves down now and slides my skirt down to pool at my ankles.

"I'm going to break you in two, and you're going to love every minute of it," he tells me before he bites down on my earlobe, sending shocks right down between my legs. I gasp and arch myself even more into him.

My last inhibitions have gone; I'm a ball of pure feeling and nerves and I need him more than I ever needed anyone or anything.

"Uncle Tony," I say, my voice a needy whimper.

"What is it, tesoro?" he asks with his lips pressed against my throat. "What do you need?"

"This... More... You," I say, unsure of which is the right answer, or if all of them are. "Please," I add meekly at the end.

His rough hands lift me by the waist and he plops me onto the bed, my head bouncing on the pillow. That makes me dizzy again and the next thing I know, he's naked and suspended on his arms above me. I'm trapped now; there's no turning back even if I wanted to.

In this small, windowless bedroom, with only a thin cot and dresser and a TV, I'm at my uncle's mercy.

And I am exactly where my body wants to be, even if my brain still has a whole host of reservations. I don't know what the alcohol did to me this time, but all I feel is warmth and the need to be touched, fucked, and ruined. Specifically by him.

Uncle Tony leans down and captures one nipple in his mouth, sucking hard and my body physically leaves the bed as I arch my back. I love it when guys play with my breasts, but none really do it.

He switches between them, and one hand massages and kneads each breast. Then that hand ventures lower, brushing against the wet curls I keep meticulously trimmed.

"So ready for me, tesoro. Tell me, how long have you wanted this? How old were you when you first realized you wanted your Uncle Tony to make you a woman?"

I whimper and shake my head. "I — I don't know." I really don't know. I'm even sure I ever have, except when Tessa mentioned it. But he's so sure, so confident, I must have and didn't realize it until now.

He grips his cock and slides it along my slick lips, coating himself and driving me crazy.

"Uncle Tony, please!" I beg. "I need it; I feel like my body's on fire."

"You want me to fuck your little pussy?" he asks. "Is that what you need?" The head pushes against my opening, not entering, just teasing.

"Ahh, yes please! Fuck me, please!" I beg.

"As you wish."

In one fast movement, he seats himself fully inside of me, the stretch and burn minimized thanks to how fucked up I am. Still, it elicits a scream, somewhere between pleasure and torment. He is so thick, it's like an airtight seal.

"It's okay, you can cry and shout all you want. No one will hear you in here," he promises.

Is that encouragement or a threat?

I have no time to wonder as he pulls out of me and slams back in so hard, the little cot rattles, and I wonder if he's going to break it. He does it a few more times, pulling his face back to watch my reaction.

"You like it like this?" he wonders. "Being held down and helpless while I fuck you into the mattress?"

Whimpering with need and desire, I nod, unable to formulate words. My mind is nearly blank now, giving way to my desperate body. His cock pounds into me, and the only sounds in the room are my moans and flesh against flesh.

Only when I feel myself nearing the edge does he speak again, "I feel you clenching around me. Come on, pretty girl. Come all over your uncle's cock."

He bites down hard on a nipple and the pain meets pleasure as I shatter beneath him and feel his hot come flooding inside me.

And after that … darkness.

* * *

My head is killing me.

That's the first thought that hits me as I slowly begin to give in to consciousness. The thing feels like it weighs more than my entire body as I struggle to open my mascara-crusted eyes. There's a dim overhead light, but even that makes my eyes feel like someone torched them with a lighter.

I'm naked.

Where the fuck am I?

I slowly sit up, but can only manage a slight reclining position. Why? I look down and see my wrists and ankles are strapped to the tiny cot I'm sleeping on and panic grips my heart. I can't breathe.

Closing my eyes tightly, I count to ten and open them again. Nope. Still here. So since it's not a dream, I need to remember what happened last night.

Tessa. The club. Fucking Trevor stealing my panties. I remember storming out and then there was a car ... I was scared...

"Uncle Tony."

The words are barely a gasp, but they act like a summoning ritual. Before I can completely wrap my mind around the things I'm trying to remember, the door to this windowless room opens and in walks my uncle. He's wearing pajama pants and nothing else. His cock is half hard and impossible to miss under the thin flannel.

"What the fuck?" The words slip out without meaning to. I still can't remember last night, but my current position gives me an idea. And I don't like it one bit.

He chuckles, shutting the door behind him. "Sleep well?"

"That's not funny!" I snap, tugging at my restraints.

"Sorry about those. Didn't want you freaking out and running off as soon as you woke up," he says, walking closer.

"Why am I here?" I ask, afraid of the answer. "Why am I restrained, and most importantly, why am I *naked*?"

"One question at a time, tesoro." He sits on the edge of the cot, uncaring that I'm nude.

What the fuck?

"You're here because I helped you lie to your mom after I found you drunkenly stumbling in the middle of the city by yourself. I gave you a place to sleep it off. Like I said, you're restrained to keep you from freaking out and running off, since I didn't think you'd remember anything from last night. And since you don't know why you're naked, I guess I was right." He gently pats my thigh and shivers run through me.

Stop it, I scold myself. *This is so wrong!* "Well, you can untie me now. I'd like to go home. Please," I add, almost as an afterthought.

His hand keeps caressing, getting closer and closer to my slightly sore pussy. Wait. Why is my pussy sore?

"Don't you want to know what you got up to last night? What you begged for?" Tony's grin is lopsided and almost feral.

"I—" I have no idea, and I can't even form a sentence. Because I'm not stupid. I was drunk and angry and now I'm naked with a throbbing slit. But … how? How could my uncle do this, even if I did beg for it?

Uncle Tony gets up and finds a remote. He clicks on the small flat-screen TV and at first, all I see is … me. Right there, as I am now. There's apparently a camera somewhere. All I do is turn my head and see it, mounted above the TV. I must have been super fucking lit if I didn't notice that.

Tony clicks something and the scene on the TV shifts from me now, to something timestamped as around one AM. The camera must either always record, or it was triggered to start when the door opened. Because there I am, in Uncle Tony's arms. He's carrying me to the bed and plops me down. I see myself spread my legs wide by accident.

There's no sound, but I don't need it as I watch, growing more and more horrified ... and a little hot, if I'm being honest. I watch my uncle tear at my clothes, watch him touch me, watch myself get on my knees and swallow his cock like a porn star.

"Stop," I whine, not sure I mean it. "I don't want to see anymore. I was drunk! I couldn't consent!" And yet I can't tear my eyes away as my uncle

bites my breasts and shoves his cock
into me on the TV.

"Oh, you consented. Vigorously,"
Tony replies. "Begging for more like a
whore on a street corner."

"Why don't I remember?" I
wonder.

"Well, you were drunk, and then I
made you … loosen up," Tony says with
a triumphant smirk.

"What did you do to me?" I ask,
terrified of the answer.

"Just a little crushed up Molly in
the vodka bottle you took out of my
glove compartment. Not enough to hurt
you, just enough to loosen your
inhibitions and let me see if you really
were as slutty as your ex made you seem
on Facebook." His hand is higher now
and my whole body feels like it's
vibrating.

I put two and two together and somehow come up with five as the last puzzle piece slides into place.

"You're the Northside Rapist!"

He chuckles. "I have never raped anyone. As that video proves. You were all over me, taking my cock like a pro. And so was every other girl I've picked up. I gave you and them opportunities to leave. The others, I even offered to call them cabs. They all stayed. Why do you think only two reported me? Because they all saw themselves being my willing plaything. Just like you, tesoro."

His index finger slips in between my pussy lips and I know what he finds there: I'm wet. My breath hitches as he strokes me lightly.

"You loved it last night, and you'll love it now, too. Because you can protest all you want, my sweet little niece, but your body speaks the truth your lips refuse to acknowledge: you want me."

"Don't do this," I beg, unsure why. He already did this. I'm watching the proof on TV. And apparently I liked it.

"Do what? Make you face reality? Tesoro, it's about time you realized you have to grow up, and I'm here to help you." His finger strokes harder, avoiding hitting my clit, but so gentle, so perfect.

Heat coils inside of me, and I want nothing more than to die. Because I'm enjoying this, and because I'm not.

He leans down and captures one of my nipples between his teeth and I moan. I know he has to feel it as my pussy clenches, because he chuckles, releasing my nipple with a pop.

Uncle Tony moves his whole body, swinging his leg over me as he moves his pajama pants down, revealing his cock. He's not even getting undressed: this is more business than pleasure for him, I think.

As he suspends himself on his arms over me, his muscles flex with the strain. Some primitive part of my brain wants to lick them, and I remind it to shut up.

And then he does the most unexpected thing a serial rapist could do: he kisses me. Now I'm sober, I can really feel his kiss. His lips are plush and soft, but his short beard is abrasive, rough against my skin without meaning to be. His tongue parts my lips and I let him. I've never been kissed like this and I don't want it to stop.

My hips arch of their own accord, and the next thing I know, he's inside of me to the hilt. I moan into his mouth and he bites my lower lip.

I don't want this.

At least, I thought I didn't want this.

Now I don't know anything.

Uncle Tony's cock isn't like the video he took of us: he moves slow and deliberate, filling me to the hilt before pulling out in slow, deliberate thrusts. My body responds, and liquid heat builds inside me.

He finally stops kissing my lips, moving down my throat and then suckling on a spot below my ear that makes me see stars. One hand moves to roll my clit between his fingers and I come undone, calling his name as my body spasms uncontrollably.

He keeps pumping through my orgasm until he bites down on my earlobe and hot come fills my insides.

Breathing hard, I realize there are tears in my eyes, and I don't know why.

Uncle Tony slowly pulls out and kisses me again. He gets up and pulls his pants up before unbuckling all four restraints. He points to a small chair in the far corner I never saw. It has clothes on it.

"You can wear those. I'll have an Uber waiting for you to take you home."

Sitting up, I rub my wrists to get some circulation back. "And if I tell them to take me to the police?"

He chuckles. "Then I have two videos of you moaning like a whore as I make you come to show them." He opens the door partway. "I know it's a lot to process, tesoro, but when you realize how much you loved it, you will come crawling back, begging for me to take you again. Mark my words."

Chapter Four

Sasha

INSIDE THE UBER home, I sit quietly, wearing the borrowed clothes that do not match my pale pink sequined clutch.

"Wild night, huh?" the woman driving asks with a conspiratorial wink in the rearview mirror.

"You could say that," I reply, not meeting her eyes in the reflection. I'm thinking 'wild' might not be the right adjective, but what do you call getting molested by your ex and drugged and screwed by your uncle in one night?

Not to mention the deadly hangover I have right now. Feels like my brain is about to pulse so hard, it oozes out of my ears. But would that be so bad? At least I wouldn't be able to remember anything at all.

Not that I really can. Whatever Uncle Tony gave me made my brain reject pretty much every major detail from the night before, but this morning is quite vivid.

I take a deep breath and lean my head back as the driver nears my house. The last thing I want to do is face my mother, but unless I learn how to teleport in about two minutes, I have no choice.

Going to pay the driver, she shakes her head. "It's on Mr. Santini's account."

How gentlemanly. Drug me, get me drunker, fuck me, restrain me, but be sure to pay for my ride home.

I go inside, slipping off my heels, and try to creep up the stairs when I hear the dreadful full name.

"Sasha Maria Santini, get your ass in here *now*!"

Mom is sitting in the living room, hair in its usual high bun and looking like she's ready to go in the office, not lounge at home on a Sunday.

"Mom, I know—"

"Do you think you get to speak right now?" She stands up, arms crossed. "It's bad enough you let those stupid girls get you drunk — illegally, might I add — but then you call your uncle and try to make him cover for you? How special do you think you are?"

Not very, as you and Trevor have always reminded me.

I remain silent, knowing better than to answer that.

"As soon as you saw the liquor, you should have come straight home! Were there drugs? There had to be drugs," she comments. "What did you take?"

"Nothing!" That I answer, despite it being a lie. But I didn't *know* I took anything, so technically not a lie. Right? "If they had anything, they know better than to tell or show me because of Daddy."

My mother hates being confronted with logic. It's a big part of why she and Daddy fought a lot. She gets these outlandish ideas and blows a paper cut so out of proportion, you'd think she'd been stabbed with a butcher knife.

"Don't have that fucking attitude with me!"

Nobody has an attitude here except you, I think. "Mom, I feel like death. Please, can I just get some water and go to sleep?"

"No, you will stay awake and watch your siblings while I go into the office. If I want this promotion, I have to put in as much manpower as I can. It's more than you deserve right now to even be allowed out of your room!" She huffs and turns away. "I have a seminar next Friday, and I will not let your insolent behavior ruin it for me!"

She leaves, slamming the door behind her, and all I can do is sink to the living room floor and cry.

* * *

I get over my tears before my siblings come downstairs, and manage to make a cup of coffee. My stomach protests, but I choke down a piece of toast so I can take two aspirin with my caffeine.

I even manage to make them lunch before Mom comes back. The second she does, she starts in on me.

"I was late because of you! You need a good, hard lesson in respect before you head off to college." She slams her purse down, then slams the chair in the kitchen, probably for absolutely no reason. "This week, you're grounded. School, and home. That's it. No friends, no nothing."

That should've pissed me off more than it did. But, frankly, I was pissed at Tessa for inviting Trevor and not telling me, pissed at Trevor for touching me without permission (again), and pissed at myself for what I let happen. I couldn't get any more pissed if I tried.

And yet, I couldn't exactly find it in me to be pissed at Uncle Tony.

Staying home sounds fan freakin' tastic.

Before I finally go to bed, I check my messages. My phone died and I hadn't had the energy to go upstairs and get my charger earlier. The first ding makes my skin crawl. Trevor. I blocked his number, but he must've gotten another one.

"That pussy still belongs to me, Sasha. And you know it. You'll be back with me soon. Count on it."

"Fuck all the way off," I mutter, deleting that and blocking the new number.

The second one is from Uncle Tony.

"I thought since you weren't all there, you might want a reminder of last night. I had fun, and I want you to see that you did, too. Come back anytime: I always have a bed open for you, tesoro. Oh, and your Daddy says hi."

The attachment is so large, I have to turn on Wi-Fi to get it. It's a video, about an hour and a half long. I know what it is. It's obvious. And yet I open it and watch anyway. Two things become abundantly clear quickly.

Number 1, I was definitely drugged.

Number 2, Uncle Tony gave me a chance to run. And instead I acted like a lustful idiot and gobbled his cock like it was a popsicle on a 100 degree day.

I lay back on my bed, feeling sick and turned on and confused.

What the Hell am I going to do?

Chapter Five

Gene

BEING A FRATERNAL twin is interesting. We don't really have the whole 'twin psychic link' or whatever identical twins do. But we are similar in other ways, despite barely looking related. Tony looks like Dad's side of the family, a dark blond-haired Northern Italian with a prominent nose and deep, green eyes that offset his olive skin. I'm darker, looking every bit the Sicilian like Mom.

One thing my brother Tony and I have in common is our taste in women. However, unlike me, Tony doesn't know what commitment means. I was married for eleven years and have two beautiful biological kids. And Sasha. Though she's not mine by blood.

Tony, on the other hand, I think his longest girlfriend lasted three months. Maybe. It's a running joke now.

Ever since I divorced Gina, he's tried to set me up on blind dates. Tried getting me to go to bars and clubs and find women to hook up with. That's not me, never has been, never will be.

Besides, in the past six months, I've been able to live vicariously through my brother's escapades with the random girls he drugs and fucks in his little "guest room", as he calls it.

I know, as a lawyer, what he does is borderline illegal, but half these girls are on drugs anyway when they go out, and the videos show explicit consent.

Drunk or not, fucked up or not, these sluts beg for it.

And it's hot as fuck to watch. Especially the next day, when they're groggy and confused and all but two were still happy to oblige his dick. Some are reluctant, but by the time he's inside, a switch flips in their eyes. You can see it.

I wasn't sure it was a good idea for him to tape everything, but it was our dad who suggested it after the first couple girls he bragged about.

"If they're on tape saying yes multiple times, they've got nothing on you," he explained.

He took a small break after the news story broke. Or, that's what he told me. Until Monday at work, when he walks into my office, Cheshire cat grin on his face.

"What'd you do?" I ask. "Or rather, who'd you do?"

"You'd never believe me if I didn't have it on video," he replies, standing in front of me, leaning on the back of my guest chair. His phone is clutched in his hand, which means he's primed and ready to show me the sordid videos.

"Lay it on me."

"I sent it to you. Enjoy. I'll shut the door and tell your assistant not to bother you." He winks at me and laughs as he does just that.

We — Tony, Dad, and me — all have separate burner smartphones we use just for the videos Tony sends. It might not get by in court, but we're still careful.

I pull that phone out of my briefcase and place it horizontally on the table in front of me. I'm a little miffed

Tony didn't take it easy like he said, but not my problem. I click on the video and it starts the usual way: him carrying a drunk but conscious young girl into the room and dropping them on the bed.

Hair is in her face and her legs are spread. No panties. I wonder if he took them, or she didn't wear any. Her head stays down as Tony rips her top off, revealing heavy, round breasts that bounce as she recoils back. My cock stirs in my lap and I rub it through the fabric of my dress pants.

Her face isn't clear as she reaches down and begins to rub Tony's cock, but before she sucks, she moves her hair out of her face in a familiar gesture I saw for years.

Sasha.

Tony's fucking the kid who's called him 'uncle' since she was five. My daughter. No matter the fact we're not blood related, she's *still* my daughter, even with her mouth wrapped around my brother's cock.

And yet I don't stop the video.

He kisses her, plundering her mouth before shoving her onto the cot. He climbs on top of her.

And I still don't stop the video.

He starts to bite and suck one breast while kneading the other. Sasha whimpers and moans like a little whore.

And my cock gets harder; I rub it absently. Still not stopping the video.

I watch Tony fuck her to the point of unconsciousness after she comes wildly. He locks her up in the restraints.

And I still don't stop the video.

It skips to what must be the next morning, as Sasha panics and tries to escape the leather cuffs, but can't. Of course not, those are buckled tight around her wrists and ankles.

Tony comes in and sits on the bed, rubbing her thigh. Telling her how she wanted it last night, even as she begs him to stop.

And yet, I don't stop the video. Instead, I pull my hard cock out and begin to stroke it.

He mounts my step-daughter again and begins to slowly thrust, shaking the cot. He kisses her wetly, passionately. I've never seen him kiss a woman like that, whether on these videos or with a girlfriend. It's sensual. It's ... almost loving.

She moves her hips and takes every stroke; her moans are like music. As she comes with a cry, tears in her eyes, so do I, staining my desk as it shoots out of me in hot, thick ropes.

The video stops and I lean back in my chair, sweat beading my brow and my heart heavy. Never once did I think of Sasha in any way except as a step-daughter. Hell, I treated her as my own biological kid; never singled her out over or under her siblings.

Since I divorced Gina, I haven't seen her much except on Facebook. And I do feel a little guilty, but she used to be a shy, quiet sixteen-year-old. When did she become the woman I saw in that video?

Recalling how she swallowed Tony's cock, I moan as my cock gives an interested twitch, despite not having nearly enough time to recover yet.

I glance at the thumbnail on the video and grimace. Since when did I become such a horrible person? And how obvious about it could I be that

Tony knew I'd get off on something that should, for all intents and purposes, make me kill him?

Shame mixes with curiosity now, wondering what Sasha feels like, really sounds like in person. She looks like her mom with her olive skin and highlighted brown hair, but her face is softer and her lips pout without plastic surgery. Would she be tighter? Would she take it in the ass, which her mother refused to do? Would she take Tony and I at the same time?

Fuck, I'm a perv. I always knew it, however I never thought I'd stoop down to this level, but here I am, and I don't really care. Now that the switch has been flipped, I can't help it.

As I tuck my cock back in my slacks and zip up, my regular cell rings. It's my ex-wife. Is she psychic? I almost don't answer, too ashamed after what I just did watching her daughter, but I pick up.

She never calls me first.

"Gene, I am so glad you picked up!" Her voice is overly perky. She wants something, which is rare. She doesn't ask for anything outside of alimony and child support.

"Good thing you didn't call five minutes ago, I was … incapacitated," I reply.

"L'Oreal wants me to go to a seminar this Friday. It's a few hours away, and will run late. I don't think bringing the kids is a good idea. Can you come stay at the house and watch them until Saturday?" she asks. "I'm excited, this is only for the top-tier. People are coming from France!"

Gina always worked, despite me making more than enough. One of the good things about her. If only she wasn't such a frigid, controlling shrew.

"Yeah, I can do that. I don't have work this weekend, and if I get any, they'll let me do it remotely," I reply. "Don't trust Sasha with the babysitting duties?"

Gina huffs. "She's grounded, and I want you to make sure she doesn't leave the house this weekend."

"What'd she do?" I wonder, glancing at the thumbnail. It's of her on her knees, Tony's cock between her lips.

"Got drunk at a friend's, then called your brother to pick her up, thinking he'd keep it from me. Not likely. He let her sleep it off and she knew she was in trouble when she got home," Gina said. "Thank God Tony is a decent person."

"Yeah, he's a peach," I mutter, trying to keep from smirking. "What time do you need me there Friday?"

"I leave early in the morning, but Caleb and Maggie don't get home until around three from the bus. Sasha takes them both to school and drives herself home. I'll be back Sunday evening."

I nod, rubbing my forehead. "Yeah, sure, I'll be there before three. I'm sure the kids will be surprised." Shit, I almost said 'happy'. That would've set her off.

She gives me a few more instructions and hangs up. I push my phone across my desk and put my head in my hands. The video keeps playing on a loop in my mind and I hope I don't do or say the wrong thing this weekend.

At lunch, it's Dad's turn to buy for Tony and me, so we go to a cafe nearby. Dad and Tony are there first, and I pause to watch how every semi-straight woman working there bends over backwards for them.

Dad might be sixty-two, but he looks closer to fifty and has a commanding presence. Most women, no matter their age, love him. I'm pretty sure he fucked a few of my college girlfriends before I met Gina. Not that I'm bitter. None of us three ever had a problem sharing anything, women included.

When I approach the table, one waitress flocks to my side. How can someone simper when asking if I want a drink?

"Gin and tonic with a twist," I reply flatly, which makes Dad roll his eyes.

"Eugene, how many times do I have to tell you, when they practically beg for it, don't deny them," he scolds.

"He never got it," Tony reminds him. "Guy looks like Chris Pine but won't take the bait."

"I don't give a fuck who I look like. I don't like 'desperate'," I explain. "I like when I have to work for it."

Tony chuckles. "Like you had to work for it with Gina, who would barely suck you off?"

Dad hums in agreement. "At least her daughter knows better."

Shit, Dad saw the video, too? Why am I surprised? He's seen all the others Tony sends over.

Tony leans back in his chair and nods. "You can say that again. I've never had a woman like her. And to be fair, I did have to work for it a little."

"You didn't feel bad?" I asked.

Tony moves his hand from side to side. "Menza menz. At first, on the sidewalk, I didn't know it was her. My first thought after I saw it was her, was to take her home. But she was so sweet and trusting and I felt her tense up when I accidentally grabbed her tit and ... that was it. There was no turning back. And I'm glad I didn't."

I smirk. "We're all going to Hell."

"Might as well have some fun before we head down then, huh?" Dad comments. "Speaking of Hell, Alderman Helios wants us to go to a party on Saturday. It might be boring, but I bet there will be some drunk housewives who hate their husbands willing to have fun."

I shake my head. "Can't. Promised Gina I'd stay with the kids till Saturday night. She's got a seminar out of town."

Tony lets out a whistle. "All alone in a house with Sasha after the other kids go to bed? Lucky fucker."

"Don't go there," I warn, but my cock likes the idea.

Tony scoffs. "I already went there. Your turn."

Chapter Six

Sasha

I'M BEING INFANTILE, but I'm not talking to Mom right now. I know, I know, I'm an adult and I should act like one. But to be fair, my mother gives silent treatments better than anyone I know. It used to drive Daddy nuts.

Honestly, I'm glad I'm not talking to her anyway, because I'm not sure how long I could keep what really happened a secret. And I'm ashamed. I'm ashamed I left the party alone and drunk like that, when I know better. But what I'm really ashamed about is that I liked it. And I've rewatched the video every night, making myself come over and over again with it before bed.

It's driving me crazy. I'm not interested in my uncle, am I? And what the fuck was with his message?

"Daddy says hi."

Did he mean *Daddy* saw the video? No way, right? He'd have killed Uncle Tony. And yet … my mind wanders.

When I was twelve, I couldn't sleep so I went to the bathroom to get some water in a Dixie cup. The master bedroom door was open, the lights dim but enough for me to see by. I couldn't see Mom, the door wasn't open that far. But I could see Daddy.

By that time, I knew what sex was in a technical way because I got my period. And I found Uncle Tony's stash of Playboy *that summer.*

However, that didn't prepare me for
what I saw, or what I heard.

Daddy was naked, turned
sideways to face the bed. He stroked a
penis that I didn't know at the time was
huge. Long and thick and veiny. I knew
looking at naked people was wrong, but
I was fascinated, staring at his dick as
it hardened before my eyes.

"Still won't let me in the
backdoor, Gina?" he asked Mom.

"Not on your life. Talk like that, I
won't let you in anywhere tonight," she
replied, sounding disgusted.

Daddy chuckled, but it didn't
sound like he was amused. More like he
was angry. He stopped stroking
himself, and his cock bobbed in the air.

"Don't be stupid, you're going to
let me in," he said. "You're going to take
my cock in your frigid cunt and like it."

I shake my head, the memory ends there. I ran back to my room as quietly as I could, forgoing my water.

At the time, I wasn't sure what he meant about the backdoor, but after getting with Trevor, I know it means anal. I don't blame Mom for not liking it. I wasn't a fan, either. At first.

Imagining Daddy's long cock pounding into my guts, I'm soaking wet again. My fingers slip between my legs, hoping to get myself off before school.

"Sasha! I'm going!" Mom's voice calls through my closed bedroom door.

"Have fun!" I vaguely recall her mentioning a seminar. Mood officially ruined, I get off my bed and walk to the door. Hopefully I can return to my imaginings after school.

* * *

I don't park in the garage when I get home, because I think we need groceries and hopefully Mom will appreciate my going to buy them with my own money.

Inside the house, I hear Caleb and Maggie laughing as I take my shoes off. I smile a little; I adore my siblings. They're not total brats like other kids, even if Maggie gets on my nerves sometimes.

"Sasha!" Caleb calls. "Come play!"

I hang up my jacket and walk into the living room still in my school uniform, pausing.

Daddy's here. Why is Daddy here?

"Hey," he says, giving me what I think is a once over. "Dinner will be delivered tonight. Pizza and lasagna, your favorite. Come sit and play." He pats the spot on the couch next to him and I nod, hating how my brain works now.

He raised you, my mind scolds me. *Stop being a whore.*

I sit down and smile. "What are you doing here?"

"Your mom has a weekend seminar. I'll be here until tomorrow night," he explains.

"Mom told us the other day," Maggie comments. "You were too hungover to listen."

"Was that last Sunday?" Daddy asks. "Your mother told me you were grounded."

I put my head in my hands and sigh. "Yeah. I am."

He shakes his head. "You were never so much of a rebel before."

"I just didn't get caught," I mutter. *In more ways than one.*

Daddy drops the subject because my siblings want to start playing a new game of Monopoly. Soon enough, two hours have passed and Caleb has beaten us all, much to his delight.

The doorbell rings and Daddy tips the driver while Maggie and I go set the table. Caleb is on cleanup duty tonight.

Daddy makes sure all three of us feel loved and valued as he asks us all questions, but mine are no longer kid stuff like classmates and after school sports. He asks me about college, my career, if I want a family one day.

"Eventually, yeah, I'd like a family. But I want to pass the BAR and work for you and Uncle Tony and Nonno."

But do I? After what happened and how I'm thinking about Uncle Tony and Daddy, is that really the best option for me?

And I realize pretty quickly, yes, that is my best option. I have a ready made job with an open place just because I'm a Santini in name, if not in blood. If I let my pussy fuck that up, I'd never forgive myself.

Daddy smiles with a gleam in his eye and says, "You've always got a space between us, Sasha." His hand squeezes my thigh and I immediately excuse myself, citing homework.

I just need to get out of Dodge.

I actually do my homework until both my siblings tell me goodnight. That's when I can't take it anymore, still feeling Daddy's hand on my thigh. I get changed into a little black silk teddy and lay on my bed, on my back, lights still on. I have a few toys I bought in the city I hide from my mother in the hollow bottom of my makeup box.

I take the lube out, too, even though I'm so wet I don't need any, as I use a decent sized dildo to tease my folds. I spread my legs and use my other hand to spread myself further.

First person to come to my mind is Uncle Tony, and how gentle yet violently he fucked me the second day, when I was still confused but horny. Gradually, he morphs into Daddy, strong hands on my thighs, that long cock nudging my ass...

Just as I'm about to try the dildo down there, my bedroom door opens without a knock and I shoot straight up in bed, the dildo flopping next to me.

Daddy stares down at me from the doorway, smirking.

"Some homework," he comments. He slips into the room and quietly closes the door behind him. In the stunned silence, the click of the lock is deafening. "What are you studying? Filthy slut 101?"

"Daddy!" I cry, but there's not much emotion in it aside from embarrassment. "What do you want?"

He walks closer, hands in his pockets. Casual as Hell. "I could hear you moaning. It was a toss up if you were sick or pleased, so I wanted to check. Is that so wrong?"

He's right in front of the bed now; I can see the outline of his cock in his gray slacks.

"I'm fine. You can go. Goodnight." I cross my legs closed, but the damage has been done. Alone the dildo at my side and the lube on the nightstand.

Daddy shakes his head. "You know, I don't think your mother would be too happy to hear what you *really* did last Saturday night."

He knows. Uncle Tony must've told him, or sent him that fucking video. Glorious.

"Are you blackmailing me?" I ask, eyes wide.

Daddy cocks his head and smiles wider. "I'm giving you a choice, Sasha. Are you going to be a good girl, or do I have to explain that you weren't hung over so much as recovering from your encounter with the Northside Rapist after going to a club you're far too young to get into legally?"

Mom would be apoplectic. She'd probably insist I live at home rather than at the dorms in college.

"Daddy, stop. Please," I beg. "You were always on my side before."

"I am on your side," he insists, sitting on the mattress. His right hand slides up my right leg and I shiver. "But you're an adult now, and you need to act like one." He uses his left hand to gently lift my chin so I'm looking him in the eye. "You didn't just break rules, you broke the law. And you need to be punished for that."

"O-okay," I stammer.

His right hand slides higher, where my inner thigh is slick with arousal.

"Tell me the truth, were you thinking about my brother while using that thick dildo in your pretty little cunt?"

A small gasp escapes at his words, but what's the point in lying? "Yes, sir." My voice is small and trembling in my ears.

"I never imagined the little girl I raised could become such a wanton whore," he comments nonchalantly. "And you're not even telling me to stop." His hand goes higher, brushing my dripping slit, and my body jerks.

"Would you?" I wonder.

He grins, looking more like Tony than normal. "No."

That one word at once makes me feel sick and excited. This is going to happen one way or another; I might as well enjoy myself, right?

"Turn over," Daddy commands. "On your stomach, ass up." He lets me go and stands up, watching and waiting for me to do as he asked.

I nod and turn over, no longer able to see anything except my headboard. I grip my pillow in my arms and wait. My nipples press to the bed, adding to the mix of sensations swirling within me.

First I hear his belt being undone. Then he lifts my nightie's hem and cool air hits my ass and pussy.

"I don't believe in spanking children, but you're not a child anymore, little cunt."

Before his words register, there's a loud snapping sound and my asscheek is on fire. He whipped me! With a *belt*!

"Daddy!" I cry in protest.

"Don't 'daddy' me, Sasha. I raised you. If anyone should get a first crack at your cunt, it should've been *me*, not my brother."

This is so sick. This is so wrong. Any sane person would call for help, or try and run. They would've gone to the cops and explained they were drugged with Molly before being fucked (raped?) by their uncle. A sane person would not hear their stepfather say these things and get even wetter.

Guess we've established I'm not a sane person.

The belt hits me again and I whimper. I never equated pain and arousal with Trevor, no matter how much he tried to make me do so. But now...

Another hit, on the other cheek this time. By the time he reaches five slaps, I feel tears in my eyes from the pain. They don't stop him; he keeps going until he hits ten and my ass burns and stings.

I whimper from pain, while my pussy throbs and drips. Betraying bitch.

Daddy's strong fingers caress along my dripping slit, dipping inside, and I gasp as they brush my swollen clit.

"Dirty girl. Who made you a whore, little one? Was it that bastard of a boyfriend?"

I nod, not wanting to open my mouth lest things I'd rather not discuss leap out.

"Guess he was good for one thing: training you to take Daddy's cock," he says. Removing his now soaked fingers from my slit, he runs them up until he gets to my rear hole.

My whole body tenses.

"Have you ever been fucked in the ass, baby girl?" he wonders.

"Yes, Daddy," I reply.

"Good slut," he praises, then drags more of my wetness around my hole before inserting one, then two fingers. He scissors them in and out, stretching me slowly. He pulls them out, and then there's a clicking sound and I hear him squirt the lube, presumably coating his cock in it.

Sure enough, I feel the slick, bulbous head pressed against my asshole and my whole body tenses up.

"Loosen up, baby girl. This is going to feel good, I promise," Daddy whispers, a hand gently rubbing my lower back as he slowly inserts just the head.

I cringe as he presses past the initial ring of muscle, then goes deeper in almost one thrust. It feels like my breath is caught in my throat from the sudden rush of pain and feeling of fullness.

"Good girl." He thrusts shallowly a few times, getting me accustomed to his size. "My brother missed out by not ruining your tight asshole. He saved it all for me." He thrusts back in all the way, and my pussy throbs even as pain radiates through me.

This is why I never said no to anal with Trevor, even if I was allowed to. I love how much it burns. It makes me feel alive. However, Daddy is much bigger than Trevor.

Daddy wraps one strong arm around my chest from the front and hauls me up so I'm basically sitting on his dick. It's even deeper inside me now. His rough wool slacks press against my wounded cheeks and thighs as he thrusts upwards, making me see stars.

"Touch yourself," he commands as his other hand begins to play with my right breast.

I do as he asks with one hand, bracing myself with the other on his leg. I'm even more soaked; the duvet beneath me is wet.

He kisses and sucks on my neck and ear as he pounds into me, making me wonder if I'll break.

"That's it, baby. Good girl. Daddy loves you, you know that. So be a good girl and take all of Daddy's cock in your sweet ass." His breath is rough as he seems to start losing control.

At his words, I want to come undone, but I'm not there yet.

"So tight. Does it hurt?" he asks.

"Y-yes, Daddy," I reply, groaning as he pushes hard inside me.

"Good. Take the pain and show Daddy how much you love him." He pinches my nipple and bites down deep into my shoulder.

That's all it takes as I rub my clit faster and come, squirting on the duvet as he keeps brutalizing my asshole.

A few more hard thrusts and he moves faster, his zipper hitting my skin with hard nips. He curses as he comes, flooding my insides with his hot come as he squeezes my breast like it's a stress ball.

We're both breathing hard, and it takes me a moment to realize I'm sobbing.

Daddy begins to kiss where he bit, then all along my shoulder and neck. He pulls out and gently lays me down, turning me so he can look at me.

His face is dotted with sweat, dark eyes glistening as he smiles. It's a mixture of sweet and predatory. I don't know what to make of it.

He leans down and kisses me, taking me by surprise. But I kiss back, noting that his face is smoother than Uncle Tony's, but his kiss is harder. He pulls away and wipes the tears from my eyes. At that moment, I truly feel as if he loves me, and not like a stepfather should.

"Goodnight, babycunt," he whispers before he turns off the light and leaves me alone in the darkened room.

Chapter Seven

Tony

"DID YOU DO it?" is the first thing I ask when Gene shows up at my house the evening after he spent the night taking care of his kids. He hasn't called or text, and now Dad and I have a bet. Dad thinks he didn't even try, I think my brother is just as depraved as I am.

I got fifty bucks riding on this. Not to mention wondering what happened. He got to see everything, I better get all the details from him.

He glances at me across the table and sips his to-go latte. I have a fucking espresso machine, and he insists on buying American shit. "Better question: why aren't you at that party with Dad, trying to fuck the mayor's wife or whoever?"

I shake my head. I'm not ready to answer that question, since I've been asking myself that all night.

"I asked first."

"I'm older."

"By three minutes!"

He starts to laugh and sips more of his drink. "I did it."

I give a cheer and can't wait to let Dad know I won the bet. "Well? You got a video of my night. I at least need a little more info than 'I did it'. Where? How? Did you get her to suck you off?"

He holds one hand up. "Calm down, man. It was in her bedroom. I teased her a little at dinner and she bolted up there. As soon as the kids were asleep, I passed by her door and heard her moaning. I went inside, pretending I was worried." He gives a small smirk. "She was fucking herself with a dildo. Looked like she was going to die when I walked in.

"She begged me to leave, and when I told her I knew where she was last weekend, she looked like she saw a ghost."

I laugh, imagining how she must've felt that I shared that video with the man she's called 'Daddy' since she was five.

"I made it easy for her: she could let it happen or I could tell Gina where she'd been — at the club, not what you did," he corrects himself. "I took my belt off and whipped her. Fuck, that ass. It looked so good covered in lashes. I should've taken a picture."

My cock gets interested as soon as he mentions blackmail, and now it's already at half mast. I rub it under my pajama pants as Gene keeps talking.

"She had lube out, which was good for her. Or I'd have caused way more pain." His free hand moves downwards, too, and I know he's as hard as I am. "Her ass was so fucking tight, she was crying, and those beautiful tits..."

"Was she an anal virgin?" I wondered. It was why I didn't take her ass when I had her. I didn't want her to be drunk and drugged if it was her first time; I wanted her to feel *everything*.

"Nope. She clammed up, but admitted the asshat she was dating, Trevor, made her do it." He took a breath. "I've fucked a ton of women. Never felt anything like I did with her. And even though she was crying in pain, I made her masturbate. When she came, she squirted like a slut." He closes his eyes, obviously lost in bliss.

I keep rubbing my cock, taking it out of my pants now.

"Yeah, me too. I've never felt anything like her. She was built to take our cocks," I admit. "Dad's gonna want a turn."

Gene laughs a little. "I almost don't want to share her."

I nod. "You and Dad are the only exceptions. A sweet pussy like that needs variety, but only the kind we can control."

"You're talking like she belongs to us," he comments.

That thought is one I've had dancing in the back of my head a while now. Hearing it said, my cock jerks.

"Doesn't she?" I ask. "We can have her. She'd let us, all three of us. You know she would."

He nods, no hesitation. "She was masturbating thinking of you, she told me. And no one comes like that without caring for the other person. That was more than sex. Even if she's too scared to admit it."

That knowledge almost makes me come like a schoolboy. I hoped she'd come to the video, violate herself remembering me violating her, but having knowledge of it is a whole other situation.

"She's why I didn't go tonight," I blurt.

"Why?"

"Because no one is going to measure up."

Gene nods. "Yeah... Yeah, that's exactly it. Everyone else is going to pale in comparison."

"She has to be ours. And she will be," I vow.

Gene nods again and stands up, still stroking himself. He comes to stand in front of me, and I reach out and replace his hand with my own, pumping us both in tandem.

He places one hand on my head and holds the table with the other to steady himself. After so many years, I'd know his cock blindfolded, just by touch, and I know he could say the same about mine.

As my brother comes and covers my face in it, it prompts one thought: just as me and him and Dad will always be together, so will she. We're family, and family loves each other forever.

* * *

Sasha

I KEEP AN eye on the news a lot more lately, after the last girl was found, but while two girls have gone missing, no bodies have turned up, and there have been no more reports of the Northside Rapist.

That doesn't mean I'm relieved or think he's stopped, however. Obviously my uncle is a disgusting pervert, and so is Daddy.

Like you haven't come over and over again because of them? my mind taunts.

Regardless if I have or haven't, it doesn't change the facts. And the facts are that they should probably both be in prison. If I had half a brain, I'd report. It's on tape that Uncle Tony drugged me, after all.

But every time I think of doing it, it makes me rewatch the video, and then I remember Daddy … and the next thing I know, I've got a dildo stuffed into me and I'm squirting all over my bed.

Maybe I'm just as bad as they are.

Mom has noticed a change in me, but she's mentioned "post-breakup" blues a few times. She's not totally wrong, I guess. Trevor's family took him on an early vacation, from what I've been told, so he's not at school, but I'm still getting random messages from him. Even if I block him, he makes a new account and tries again.

So that's bothering me, but not as much as the memories. Memories of the shit I let him do to me and hated, and memories of Daddy and Uncle Tony doing nearly the same things, yet I got off on them.

What was the difference? The illusion of choice they both gave me? Is that all it took to make me go from helpless victim to willing participant?

I don't even know anymore. I'd like to yeet my brain from my head. And my heart from my chest.

It's graduation day now, one I was looking forward to for ages. Probably since middle school. But I know they'll both be there. They were there for every other event in my life, no way they'll miss this. Mom would totally know something was up.

And … some not so small part of me wants to see them. While I'm angry and concerned, I also felt things with them I never felt before. Things I only read about in those dirty dark novels on my Kindle.

I'm ashamed, I'm confused, and I hate it.

Once we get to the high school, Mom, Caleb, and Maggie take their seats, and I scurry away into the back of the auditorium, where all the seniors are. For the first time, I'm glad I was .2 short of being valedictorian. I do not want to stand up there and be watched as I make a speech.

The principal directs us to our seats at the front of the auditorium, while the pomp and circumstance begins.

Eventually, the principal begins calling us up, one by one. By the time he reaches "Santini, Sasha," the place is more than half empty.

I take my diploma and can't help but laugh as my family bursts into raucous cheers and whistles as I shake the principal's hand. We always are the loudest and I love it.

Riding the high of graduating and being so close to my dream career, I temporarily forget about my worries as I hug everyone in my family. Neither Daddy or Uncle Tony say a word.

I haven't seen Nonno in a long time, and am one happy girl when he sweeps me up in his arms. He admittedly had Daddy and Uncle Tony when he was young, so he is only now sixty-two, and handsome as Hell. Think Alan Rickman in *Gambit*. I spy a few moms staring at him and at Uncle Tony and Daddy, too. Knowing them, they're collecting phone numbers.

Daddy caters the after graduation party with my cousins — who are pretty distant, but I grew up with most of them, and some have kids my siblings' ages — and our house is packed.

I feel truly happy for the first time in a while.

Someone taps my shoulder and I see it's Nonno. "Can we talk where it's quieter?"

I nod and follow him out onto the porch. The early summer breeze is wonderful and I watch the last rays of the sun as it vanishes in the west.

"I wanted to discuss a permanent paid internship," he begins, sitting on the porch swing and inviting me to sit, which I do. "It's known that you have a place at the family firm, and I want to be the one who trains you. Your chosen college is the whole family's alma mater, so I don't see why the Dean won't allow it."

My eyes widen and gratitude fills me. "Oh, seriously, Nonno? No joke?"

He smiles softly. "No joke, piccolina. We love you and don't want to lose you."

That sounds sort of weird, but I understand a little. If I interned elsewhere, I could leave for a different law office. That would be a horrible betrayal.

"I'm not going anywhere, Nonno, I promise," I say, placing my hand on his between us. "We're family." *Can you remind your sons of that?* I wonder.

"Good girl." He slowly moves my hand, and I half-wonder what the Hell he's doing before I feel fabric beneath my palm. Fabric … and a hot, hard cock.

I close my eyes, hoping it's a bad dream or a mistake, but as he maneuvers it so I begin to rub him, I know it's a deliberate reality. And yet I don't pull away.

"Nonno," I plead, still not looking at him.

"Shh, be a good girl for me like you were for my boys," he whispers, leaning closer and biting my earlobe. "You do want to prove yourself, don't you? Being adopted and not blood, we have to be sure you're as invested as we are."

Why does that sound like he's fucked Daddy and Uncle Tony?

"I am. Please stop," I whine. But my hand moves of its own accord even as he guides it. And I wonder, is he long like Daddy or thick like Uncle Tony?

He lets my hand go and wraps that arm around me, pulling me close as I keep caressing his clothed cock. Hot breath caresses my ear again, and then he licks and sucks on my neck.

"Oh, bella piccolina," he whispers, "they were right: everything about you is perfect. Like you were made just for us." He moves, and I take my hand from his cock. "Be good. We'll meet up in a couple of weeks, yeah?" He kisses the top of my head before going to his car, like this was a normal, everyday situation.

What the Hell have I gotten myself into? And why am I … happy about it?

I stay seated and put my head in my hands, trying to make sense of everything, when the front door squeaks as it opens.

"There you are, tesoro. Did my dad leave without saying goodbye?" Uncle Tony asks.

At his voice, something in me snaps and I leap up, uncaring about the size difference, and land a punch to his nearly rock hard abdomen. He remains still, smirking down at me, completely unfazed. Prick.

"You ruined everything!" I shout. "Why didn't you leave me alone? Why'd you have to show Daddy and Nonno that fucking video? You saw it was me that night on the sidewalk, you should've just taken me home! Now all the men who were supposed to protect me have — have—"

He crosses his arms and asks, "Are you done, kid? Or am I supposed to wait until you figure out what you want to say?"

"No! Don't patronize me, damn it!" I cry. "And to top that off, you killed someone!"

His eyes widen at that. "Wait, what?"

"Don't 'what' me! You know exactly what I mean."

"Pretend I contracted amnesia, sweetheart. Who did I kill?"

"Two days after you took me, a girl wound up dead. Her body was dumped in an alley in Wicker Park. They're crediting the Northside Rapist. In other words, you." I mimic his stance. Should I be more terrified that I'm confronting a murderer? Probably.

Now he moves, holding his hands out as if to plead with me. "I never killed anyone, tesoro. Whoever did that was not me. I don't do anything illegal. I get consent, just like you consented. And I haven't fucked anyone since you."

I was about to believe him until he added that line in. "You know, I thought you at least respected my mind if not my body. Don't try to lie to me like that. You fuck anything under twenty-five that comes your way."

He laughs, head thrown back, eyes closed. I want to bite his throat, then hate myself for the thought.

"Tesoro, please believe this: I didn't kill anyone. That's not me on the news, the police just want to think so because of the location." He steps closer and places large, warm hands on my shoulders. His usually mirthful eyes are serious now. "It's. Not. Me."

And I do believe him. I shouldn't, but something inside me demands it.

"Please be careful. Please. I've never hurt anyone, and I wouldn't have started after you especially," he says, giving my shoulders a squeeze.

Before I can answer, the door opens again and Daddy steps out.

"Having fun without me?" he asks, then sees Uncle Tony's dour expression. "What happened?"

"A girl got raped and murdered. And the news or cops or both are saying I did it," Uncle Tony replies, not taking his eyes from me.

"Good thing you haven't taken anyone down there just in case, then," Daddy says, and it gives me pause.

Was this orchestrated, or was Uncle Tony telling me the truth? How can I know? How can I trust any of them again?

Daddy comes behind me and I'm sandwiched between them. My knees tremble and it takes all my strength not to lean back into him like I want to. I feel … safe here. How can I feel safe with them?

"Baby girl, listen to us and know we love you," Daddy murmurs, placing a kiss to the top of my head. "I know you're confused, and it's okay. We'll give you time to see what you need — what you want — is right in front of you. And behind you." He chuckles and then moves away.

"I'm not yours. I don't need this — whatever this is!" I insist.

Uncle Tony answers by pulling me in for a tight hug, and I'm not sure what to do. By the time I try to decide, he pulls away anyway and walks off into the night.

I sigh and sit back down on the porch swing, running my hands through my hair.

My life is a fucking soap opera.

Chapter Eight

Sasha

HAVEN'T HEARD from anyone in my family for two weeks. And while I want to be able to intern at the family firm, I'm kinda glad. After my graduation, I was left with more questions about them and myself.

I want answers, but what are the questions? And if I deny them and deny what my body clearly wants, can I still work with them? I want to impress my stepfather especially, but at what cost? My dignity? My morals? My body? My sanity? Then again, I don't have much of that left, do I?

Taking a shaky breath, I leave my bed where I've been laying and take my wicker tote from the bottom of my closet. It has everything I need for the yearly family pool party, and there's no way I can cancel unless I fake being sick. Which I don't want to do in case Nonno calls me in for the internship. Mom will be suspicious then if I suddenly jump up well the day after playing sick.

Mom doesn't even notice I'm quiet on the car ride there, because Caleb and Maggie are chatting excitedly about seeing the cousins again and going to swim. She's probably thanking God that I'm not talking, too.

"Anthony isn't going to be there, so you can stop worrying," Mom pipes up. Anthony is Nonno. He named Tony after himself, and Daddy after *his* father.

"What?" I ask, shaking myself from my reverie.

"I figured you were worried about the potential internship. He won't be there, had a client with some emergency, according to Gene."

I pause and bite my lower lip, a twinge of something dark in my belly that Daddy was talking to Mom. *Oh my God, stop it!* I scold myself. *You are not jealous of your own mother.*

"That's good to know," I finally reply as we pull up to Uncle Tony's mansion. Caleb and Maggie rush out, carrying their individual bags but not waiting for us. I smile at them, remembering when I was that innocent. Even at thirteen, Maggie is still more innocent than I was at her age.

Uncle Tony's house looks exactly the same as it had when he brought me here that night, two weeks ago. It feels like it has been only hours as all the fuzzy memories come rushing back.

While there are a few people milling about inside, the party is outside. We've done this so many times, it's rote: get in, go to a guest room to change into our bathing suits, put on sunblock, get outside and mingle. Uncle Tony will alternate between hanging out and manning the grill — wagyu beef burgers and Vienna dogs are the standard, though he makes other things, too.

We'll meet new people, sometimes famous people, but we're not allowed to gawk at them. Even when my favorite baseball players were there a few years back, I was polite and only shook their hands. My brother, on the other hand, was speechless and absolutely adorable.

I immediately see the new first round pick of the local NFL team talking to the team's former head coach, and two actors on big crime shows are in the pool.

I can't help but smile: my life might be confusing as Hell, but I wouldn't trade it for the world.

Daddy comes right up to us, greeting first Mom, then me. I can't help myself as I run my hands down his muscular, tanned back. He'd fucked me clothed, and now I get to take a look at him with new eyes. What's the phrase? DILF? Yeah, definitely a DILF.

"Bartender is in the usual place, and the closest neighbors are on vacation, so there's no curfew," he says happily. "No one will complain about the noise, unlike a couple years back. And you two relax. I'll keep an eye on the kids."

He squeezes my shoulder and walks off while Mom makes a face. "I know he's usually nice, but never that nice. Must have a girlfriend," she mutters.

He better not, a small voice in my head grumbles, but I shut her up pretty quick.

I scan the party for Uncle Tony, who's lounging on one of the numerous comfy chairs set around the pool. He's only wearing a speedo and looks every inch the Mediterranean model. And he's not alone. Seated next to him on a chair she had to have dragged over to be so close is a gorgeous blonde woman. She's clad in a tiny red string bikini that I am convinced only stays upright because her silicone breast implants are so big, they float on their own.

No hate — if that's what she wants, good for her. A part of me just wants her to take those balloons away from my uncle. Now.

You said you didn't want him, my mind scolds. *Did you think he'd pine for you? You were a conquest, not a permanent option. And you won't be anything more, to him or anyone.*

Shut up, shut up, shut up, I think. Those words aren't mine, they're Trevor's. He told them to me many times over the course of our three and a half year relationship. But a large part of me believes him.

"Sasha!" Uncle Tony calls, waving at me. Balloon Girl next to him gives me a little wave too, as if I care.

He obviously expects me to go greet him, so I do just the opposite. I slip out of my silk purple cover up, revealing a matching bikini with push-up cups. Giving him a little wave, I dive into the pool.

As the cool water washes over me, I feel some of the frustration inside melt away. Not all of it, but a good amount. I surface and wipe the water from my face, glancing over at Uncle Tony, whose eyes are trailed on me. Without acknowledging him further, I begin to play a horrible game of water basketball with some of the little kids.

When I'm done, I herd them out to get some food, still avoiding Uncle Tony. Now Daddy is the one looking at me, then at his twin, with an obvious *what the fuck* look on his face.

I give him a little shrug and turn away to eat. If they meant anything they said, they'd talk to me. At least. Uncle Tony definitely wouldn't have a woman glued to his side. They got what they wanted out of me, and realized they couldn't manipulate me further.

For a second, I allowed them to warp my mind with whatever sick games they play. I'm sure it started because Uncle Tony drugged me, making my mind more susceptible to their advances.

I learned that while listening to Daddy and Nonno planning a defense case when I was about twelve.

Fuck, I'm so stupid to have entertained the twisted ideas they were putting in my head. But I need to get them both alone tonight and tell them one thing: I am going to work for them, I deserve it. And they can keep their cocks to themselves.

As evening descends, fairy lights all around the pool and backyard light up, giving the place an ethereal glow. Some people leave, while others keep drinking. I spy Caleb asleep, curled up on a lounge chair. Looking at Maggie, she's probably not far behind.

Sure enough, Mom approaches. "I want to get them home."

I nod. "Let me go grab their stuff. I want to stay; I have to talk to Daddy and Uncle Tony about my internship, and I'd rather do it when they're tipsy." I smirk. "You know Daddy would give me anything after he had a few beers in him."

Mom rolls her eyes. "Yeah, I remember. Okay, just let me know if you're staying here or getting an Uber."

I promise, and she reminds me not to drink. She doesn't need to worry: I have to keep my wits about me tonight.

As I head into the house, Uncle Tony grabs me by the arm. Balloon Girl is still attached at his side, now with her eyes a little unfocused from liquor.

"Tesoro, I haven't had a second to see you today," he says, eyeing me up and down.

I stand a little straighter, making sure my breasts stick out as much as possible. They might not be a match for his current conquest, but at least mine can't be used as floatation devices.

"Who's your girlfriend?" I ask, crossing my arms.

"I'm Erika," she slurs with a giggle.

"Not my girlfriend," Uncle Tony says at the same time, earning him a demonic glare from the girl.

"Well, of course, I should've remembered: you get tired of women after you fuck them, don't you?" I reply. "Anyway, I need to speak to you and Daddy. Alone."

Uncle Tony gloweres at me and says, "Fine. When the guests leave. No one is staying overnight."

That doesn't go over well with Erika, who huffs and stalks away.

"Oops, didn't mean to cockblock you," I tell Uncle Tony as I walk off, not waiting for him to reply.

I don't mingle outside as the night wears on. Instead, I remain in my bikini and cover up, reading in the living room. Uncle Tony only reads nonfiction, so I find a true crime novel and settle in.

I get so engrossed, I don't notice I'm not alone until I'm bodily yanked from my seat. The book drops to the floor with a thunk as I stare into Daddy's angry eyes. Uncle Tony stands off to the side, arms crossed, with a little smile on his face.

"Well, little girl, you've been quite the brat today, haven't you?" Daddy asks. His hand is tight on my arm, but stops just short of bruising. I don't think I could handle him bruising me like Trevor used to.

"I haven't done anything," I protest.

"You've ignored us both, and then called me a manwhore in front of that poor bimbo who just wanted a good fuck," Uncle Tony pointed out. "Too bad I had no intention of using her that way. But still, you didn't know that."

"Okay, I'm sorry!" I say, meaning it. "I was deliberately being a bitch, but I need to talk to you guys now. Seriously."

"Sorry, little one, but you don't get to ask anything of us after your behavior," Daddy says. "You have a lot of apologizing to do tonight." He lets my arm go and slides the cover up down my shoulders, letting it drop to the floor. In one fast movement, he has my bikini top undone, letting my breasts tumble out as he throws the fabric somewhere.

"Daddy!" I protest.

He kneads my breasts and bites his lip. "I wish I was your real daddy. I'd love to be able to say I made these beautiful tits as I watch you bounce on the cock that created you."

Oh God, that sends all sorts of mixed emotions through my whole body and all I can do is make a noise somewhere between a gasp and a whimper.

Uncle Tony chuckles as he comes behind me, tugging the bottoms down to pool at my ankles. "I think our little baby slut liked that idea. You'd be a daddy's girl in more ways than one." His fingers find my slit and he adds, "She's wet already."

"So, here's what's going to happen: you're going to be very, very good for us tonight, and then if we're satisfied, we'll see about talking with you," Daddy says.

Can I say no? Do I want to say no? With Trevor, those answers were 'no' and 'yes', respectively. With them, I think they might be reversed, but I can't know unless I try.

"No," I say, barely above a whisper. Fuck, even I don't believe me.

"If anything you guys told me is even half true, you'll let me speak first."

Uncle Tony runs a hand through my still damp hair. "All right then, you have two minutes. Speak."

"I want that internship, and I don't want it to be on the condition I have to fuck any of you," I say, looking Daddy in the eye. "I want it because I deserve it."

Daddy laughs, and Uncle Tony joins him.

"Tesoro, you've had a place in the firm since you told us you wanted to be a lawyer," Uncle Tony says.

"The fact that we want you to belong to us means absolutely nothing in terms of your future job," Daddy adds. He reaches out and touches my breasts again. "And I hope you don't just want to work with us because our cocks fit so perfectly inside of you."

When I find myself speechless trying to formulate a response, Uncle Tony chuckles and gently kisses my bare shoulder.

"Is that enough for you?" he asks. "You belong to us, but get the job because you're worth it even with your legs closed?"

"I — I never agreed to this," I say, feeling my resolve slipping. "You and Daddy and — and Nonno... It's not right!"

"Why? I never adopted you, and I'm not married to your mother," Daddy says. A lone finger caresses my cheek. "If you want us, baby girl, you can have all three of us. We'll adore and cherish you for the rest of your life."

"We already discussed it," Uncle Tony interjects. "You were made for us, and no matter how we met, it's what we become that matters."

"But why?" I ask abruptly. "Why me?"

"Why not you?" Daddy asks. "You're intelligent, gorgeous, kind, and look how perfectly you fit between us. When Dad gets in the mix, it will be even more perfect."

"Don't fight it," Uncle Tony whispers, hand going to my pussy again. "Let us love you the way you deserve."

At that, I lose all my defensiveness. I desperately want what they say to be true. I want their love. All of them. Whatever this is, whatever this could be, I want it. I need it. Nothing has ever felt so right as where I stand right now.

"What about jealousy?" I ask.

"There is none, not between us, and there never will be," Daddy says. "But if you even look sideways at another man, that's a different story."

I shake my head, running one hand along Daddy's muscular chest and the other grasps Uncle Tony's bicep.

"I want to be where I feel safe," I whisper.

"We'll keep you safe," they both vow at the same time. Uncle Tony adds, "And so will your grandfather."

Daddy taps my hand resting on his warm skin. "Upstairs, little one. Now."

"Yes, sir," I say softly and begin mounting the large staircase, but once I reach the landing, I'm not sure where to go. That little door at the end of the hall where Uncle Tony took me the first time?

Behind me, one of them prods at my bare butt. "My bedroom, tesoro," Uncle Tony says. "Let's go."

I enter, glancing around at the gigantic blue and white four poster bed, dresser, and electric fireplace.

I don't have time to think as Daddy steps in front of me and leads me to the bed. I get a gentle push and sit at the edge, while the two of them stand before me.

Daddy and Uncle Tony both drop their swim trunks, both already half hard. I hadn't been able to see Daddy before; he took me from behind. Now I can see his long, veiny cock, and it looks just how my mind remembers it from all those years ago.

Silently, I slide down to my knees and take them both in each hand, giving little experimental pumps. If they're not going to direct me, I'm going to take matters into my own hands ... literally.

"Good girl," Uncle Tony says. "Have you ever had two guys at once?"

I shake my head. "Never."

Daddy chuckles. "This is going to be fun. Get us all the way hard now, little cunt."

I shiver at the moniker. Trevor used to call me awful things, but he meant them. Daddy and Uncle Tony transitioning from cute pet names to 'cunt' is the exact opposite: they call me that because they love me. Not because they want me to think less of myself.

Leaning forward, I lick the tip of Daddy's cock and he moans. Making sure I'm still stroking Uncle Tony, I dip my head and suck him deeper.

He grabs me by the back of my head and suddenly I'm pushed down on Uncle Tony's cock. Easily, as if it's the most natural thing in the world, I loosen my muscles and let the two of them move me from cock to cock, controlling who I suck and for how long.

I close my eyes and enjoy it, knowing I'm giving them pleasure and they have control of the situation. It's … blissful.

"Get up," Daddy commands.

I stand and watch as he lays in the middle of the bed, beckoning me towards him.

From behind, Uncle Tony lifts me as if I weigh nothing and places me on top of Daddy, straddling him. The tip of his cock presses against my belly, the shaft lightly brushing my swollen clit.

"Good girl," he says again. "Slide down on me. Let me feel your pretty little cunt grip me."

I do, feeling him slide smoothly inside me. He goes deep, pressing farther than Trevor or Uncle Tony and I whimper, afraid to go down any more.

Daddy grips my hips and pulls me the rest of the way, causing me to cry out and nearly crash into him. I put my hands on either side of his head, breasts dangling, like it was intentional.

"Better. Fuck, you really do fit me perfectly," he praises. "Bounce, babycunt. Show Daddy how much you love him."

I begin to move, not used to this position as much, and Daddy rocks his hips, meeting me halfway as he drives himself deep within me. It hits me that neither he nor Uncle Tony asked if I'm on the pill. I am, but they don't know that.

Just as I lose myself, wondering if they wanted to get me pregnant, I feel something slick against my ass and yelp a little, causing them both to laugh.

"It's all right, it's just me," Uncle Tony says, kissing the back of my neck as he works his thick cock into my tight hole. "Fuck you're tight. Hold her still, Gene."

Daddy does so, holding me flush against him as Uncle Tony gets through the first tight ring of muscle. I cry out; he didn't stretch me first at all.

"It hurts!"

"I know," Uncle Tony says, pressing a soothing hand on the small of my back. "But you'll take the pain for me, won't you, tesoro?"

I nod and cry again as he moves further, and finally, with one hard thrust, is all the way inside me.

I've never been double stuffed, and it feels uncomfortable yet right. These two cocks were meant to be inside of me, making me nearly airtight.

After taking a moment, they both tighten their grips on me and begin a brutal pounding from both ends at once. They're perfectly in sync, and I wonder if they've shared a woman before.

Eventually, I stop thinking altogether as my brain begins to fill with nothing but pleasure and pain. No one speaks, the only noise is guttural grunts and my cries and flesh against flesh.

Pleasure and pressure builds inside me, and I know I'm close. My

hands clutch Daddy's shoulders, and I
dig my nails into his flesh.

"That's it, my little whore," he
says. "Come. Come for us while we
destroy your pretty little holes."

And I do, shouting unintelligible
words.

They keep pounding, coming
almost at once in both holes, the hot
stickiness traveling out of my holes and
down my thighs.

Uncle Tony pulls out of me first,
and the pain returns for a second after
he's out. Then Daddy gently lifts me
from his lap, laying me next to him in
the bed.

I'm blissed out, trying to catch my
breath and tame my pounding heart as
the bed dips on my other side.

Uncle Tony leans over with a wet
cloth and cleans me up, then leans over

and does the same to Daddy before tossing it aside.

He flops down on the bed, and both he and Daddy wrap their arms around me, kissing my face, lips, and neck.

And for the first time in years, I fall asleep feeling perfectly safe, happy, and loved.

Chapter Nine

Sasha

WAKING UP IN a strange bed is never a good experience. It takes me a few minutes after opening my eyes to remember last night. I expect to feel ashamed or something, but all I feel is the same joy from last night, the same peace.

"You're up."

I jump and glance at Daddy in the bedroom doorway.

"I called my dad, we're to meet him at the office today," he continues with a smile. "He has a surprise for you, little one. I had my assistant bring you clothes, they're in the bathroom. Shower and come meet us downstairs." He blows me a kiss and closes the door.

I lay there in pure bliss for another few seconds before getting out of bed to do as he said. I wince in pain; Uncle Tony did a number on my ass. But the hot shower does wonders for every ache I have.

They were so sweet; they had clothes brought for me, hair products, body wash, and a fluffy robe. The clothes are professional/casual: a white silk blouse, grey plaid pleated skirt that comes to just above my knees, and a matching blazer. There are even stiletto pumps in my size.

However, there aren't any panties.

Interesting.

I head downstairs to the dueling smells of smoke and bacon. Uncle Tony is cooking, and Daddy is watching the weather in the large, open plan living room/kitchen combo, sipping coffee.

"Good morning," I call, now a little tentative the morning after.

I didn't need to be. Both men drop what they are doing to kiss me in greeting, and all I want is to take them both back upstairs to fuck and cuddle all day.

"You look beautiful," Uncle Tony comments. "Come have breakfast. We have to meet Dad at eleven-thirty."

"Thank you. For breakfast and the clothes and soap and ... everything," I say, taking his large hand in mine.

Daddy leans over and kisses the top of my head. "Non c'è problema. Anything for you."

While I eat some bacon and fruit with a good, strong espresso, Daddy turns back to the news while checking his phone. Uncle Tony loads the dishwasher. It's so nice and normal and domestic. It feels like it's always been this way, and is always supposed to be this way.

Until something breaks my little bubble of happiness.

"Fuck. Tony!" Dad yells. "Look at this!"

Nosy as I am, I follow too, wondering what's wrong.

The news has a breaking news update. The newscaster looks dour as he stands outside an alley downtown.

"We regret to inform you that the breaking news we reported at 5am has been confirmed: a new victim of the Northside Rapist has been discovered.

Her name, we are just learning now, is Erika Black, a local model."

A picture of Balloon Girl from yesterday fills a small part of the screen, and I completely tune out what the reporter is saying.

"Fuck fuck fuck my life," Uncle Tony says. "I gave her my card with my address when I met her. She probably still fucking had it on her."

"But you couldn't have killed her," I point out.

"Doesn't matter. The cops and DA hate this family," he explains. "They're gonna be overjoyed to implicate me in this." He sighs and runs a hand through his already unruly hair. "I hope you really believe me now: I couldn't have killed Erika, and I didn't kill that girl four weeks ago, either."

Daddy shakes his head. "Sasha and me and a few other people saw her leave while you stayed. Even if they don't believe us, there are at least four other people who can corroborate your alibi," he says, going into work mode. "And you have no connection to the other dead girl."

I wring my hands, wondering something but afraid to say it. However, I can't control my mouth. It's an Italian thing, I guess.

"If someone is trying to frame the Northside Rapist, there's a chance they know who you are. This could be personal. And that person must've been at your party yesterday, or stalking the house."

Uncle Tony sighs and cups my face with shaky hands. "Tesoro, while I adore your intelligence, right now I wish you were nothing more than a dumb bimbo." He releases me and continues, "You're right. I'll check the security tapes on my laptop once we get to the office today and see if anyone followed her or was hanging around."

"Is there anything I can do?" I ask, looking between them.

"Right now, no, but if I do get pegged for this, we'll have a few tasks for you," he replies.

Daddy kisses me softly, whispering, "Such a sweet little thing."

Uncle Tony stares blankly at the TV, which is now showing a commercial for Empire flooring. "This is my punishment for what I've been doing," he mutters.

"No it is not!" I counter, hands on my hips. "Uncle Tony, you might've persuaded me more than necessary, but you didn't force me. And I bet you didn't force anyone before me. I've been raped, I'd know if that's what happened."

There's a beat of pure silence before I realize what I admitted out loud.

"Excuse me?" Uncle Tony asks.

"Who the fuck hurt you?" Daddy wonders.

For a second, I want to rewind time, but I can't. I have to move forward, and that means not lying to the men who love me.

Crossing my arms, I mutter, "Trevor."

"I knew that motherfucking figlio di puttana was no good!" Uncle Tony cries, kneeling in front of me. "Why did you never say anything? You know we would've killed him."

He's not kidding, they literally would've killed Trevor.

I shrug. "I dunno. I should've, but at first I thought I was making a big deal about nothing. Then ... before our last breakup ... he threatened Maggie. So I called his bluff and left him. That's why I drive them to school, to make sure he doesn't do anything." I take a shaky breath, trying not to cry. But I'm not sad, I'm relieved. This is the first time I ever told anyone what went on all four years of high school. It's like saying one thing led to a wide open door of word vomit.

"My first time with him — my first time ever — I got scared and chickened out, but he didn't let me go. He told me I promised, and crying wouldn't help. That I'd like it once I took the stick out of my ass. And ... I stayed because ... I came. So I figured he was right and I was just a bitch.”

Daddy sits on the couch and pulls me into his lap. Uncle Tony sits next to him and holds my legs.

“It continued. But because I let it happen and didn’t put up much of a fight, how could I report him without people telling me I gave in, so I consented? Every time I’d break up with him, he’d tell me these awful things so I’d go back. And I always did. But this last time...”

I trail off and Daddy caresses my hair.

“It’s okay, you can stop,” he says.

But I need to get it out.

“Daddy, remember a few months ago I fell while taking a walk, and my jaw hit a rock? You paid for me to get an implant for the tooth that fell out?”

He nods, his grip tightening.

"Trevor hit me when I called him out for threatening Maggie. I never fell. And that was when I called it off."

At that, I bust into tears and both men hold onto me until I quiet. It's a weight gone to have told someone, and even more of one to be able to use my experience to validate Uncle Tony.

"I will kill him," Uncle Tony says calmly, as if he's stating he's going to buy milk. "But first he'll wish he was never born."

"Don't bother. It's over. All he can really do is message me bullshit. Right now, we have to focus on you and make sure no one thinks you're a rapist," I say.

Daddy kisses the top of my head. "We'll table this, but not for long. Deal?"

I nod; it's better than nothing.

Daddy dries my eyes and when he's done, Uncle Tony reminds us that we're going to be late.

"Wait, did anyone let Mom know where I was?" I ask as I climb into the backseat of Daddy's Escalade.

"I let her know you were staying here so we could take you to see about the internship today," Uncle Tony replies.

"Thank you. I was worried she'd call me in a fit," I reply.

"We try to avoid Gina's wrath here," Daddy says, and Uncle Tony guffaws.

It's not long before Daddy parks in the underground lot of the high rise the law offices are located in. My family owns the building, and they rent some levels out to other businesses, but the top forty are for the firm.

Nonno and his late brother first rented space here right out of law school. They came to America in the early 1960s when they were little kids and they were the first people in their family to attend college. They built everything up to become the amazing and formidable firm they are today.

I've been here countless times since I was four and Mom began dating Daddy; I know this place like the back of my hand. But I've never been so antsy and excited as I ride in the elevator with Daddy and Uncle Tony. If I'm right, I'm about to take the first step into making my dreams come true.

Before we exit the elevator, I ask, "You're sure Nonno is okay with ... all this?"

"You mean the three of us sharing you? Of course," Uncle Tony assures me.

They walk ahead of me into the offices, which are empty. No one works on Sundays unless there are big cases. If anyone comes in, it's to organize files and the like so they have one less thing to do on Monday.

The top floor houses only their three offices, plus space for their assistants.

Daddy knocks on Nonno's door and goes in without a reply. I've been in all three offices, and while things get updated, little changes. The large oak desk dominates the room, and there's a low coffee table with two small armchairs and a loveseat surrounding it. A bookcase with law books and a mini fridge round out the room.

Nonno is at his desk, looking over some papers. He looks up when we walk in and his green, more like hazel, eyes twinkle. "I was beginning to think you'd be late. Boys, Sasha. I assume you know why you're here."

I nod. "I hope so, sir."

"I worked out a deal with your future Dean. You will be allowed an internship here from freshman year on; however, we can't pay you until junior year. It's a rule they can't break for donor reasons and whatnot." He stands and hands me the paperwork he was just looking over. "Read these over and sign where indicated. Judging by my boys' faces, there's something they need to discuss with me, isn't there?"

He crosses his arms and stares them down, insanely intimidating. If he looked at me like that, I'd do anything he asked. And I have a funny feeling that will happen sometime extremely soon.

They go sit at Nonno's desk and I can overhear them talking about the news that morning and my theory about someone stalking Uncle Tony.

I look over the few sheets of paper that comprise the internship contract. They state when I can be paid, my future duties as an intern, and the assurance of a position as long as I pass the BAR exam after law school. I smile to myself as I fill out the blank spaces on the form.

My life — my future — has arrived.

I steal a glance at the three Santini men talking intently at the desk and bite my lip. I have no idea how any of this happened. It feels like an insane whirlwind, but right now I have men who adore me and make me feel like the most amazing creature in existence.

That on top of the job security makes me think that the time I suffered at Trevor's hands was all for something: it led me here, however indirectly.

Uncle Tony gets up and leaves, only to come back a few minutes later with his laptop. "I wanted to access my security camera footage on the building's internet," he explains as he sits in one of the armchairs across from me. "Do any of you remember the date the first body was found?"

"May 25th," I say quickly. "The Monday after I was at your house."

He smirks and types on his laptop. "God, I love a smart slut."

"Semantics, Anthony," Nonno scolds. "She's not *a* slut, she's *our* slut. There's a difference."

"Motherfucker!" Uncle Tony cries. "The same car goes by not once,

173

not twice, but three fucking times! The first time it followed me the night I picked you up—" he points to me "—the second time was the day you went home, and it stuck around for ten minutes before driving off. Finally, yeah, it was outside yesterday. I see it drive off after I put Erika in an Uber." He types furiously. "I can only get a partial plate, but I have a make and model."

"All right," Daddy says. "We'll run it and present it to the police, tell them you saw it drive off after sitting there all day when Erika left. Set a precedent for stalking, and you're off the hook."

Nonno comes and sits next to me, a warm hand on my back. "You figured that out, didn't you?"

I nod, blushing but proud.

"My brilliant piccolina." He leans in and kisses my face, close to my jaw, then lower on my throat. "Our business has concluded, and I'm going to order us all a nice lunch, but first I have to punish my sons."

"Why?" I wonder.

He chuckles, hands now roaming down my blouse, picking away at the buttons there. "They have each been balls deep inside you twice, while I have yet to touch you. That's certainly no way to show respect, is it?"

"No, sir," I say.

"So they can watch and masturbate if they want to, but they're not allowed to touch you for the rest of the day. I will have you now, and later, all to myself." He kisses me again as he slides the blazer and blouse from my shoulders. Next goes my bra, and I close my eyes as strong fingers knead my tits, then pinch and twist at my nipples.

I moan; there's something to be said about how well older men fuck. All he's done is kiss me and play with my breasts and I'm soaked.

"Get on your knees and suck my cock, nipotina," he commands.

I nod and do as he says, while Daddy comes and sits next to Uncle Tony. Both of them have tents in their trousers already. Nonno sits where he is, not moving to undo his fly or belt. That's obviously my job, to be full-service for him.

I do so, releasing a half hard cock as thick as Uncle Tony's, and a bit longer. I get to work right away, knowing Nonno won't let me off easily. As with everything else in his life, he's going to expect perfection.

He doesn't thrust, doesn't guide me. It's my job to keep him hard and interested, and I do, until he finally yanks me by the hair and pulls me to stand. The hand now goes under my skirt and between my legs, finding my swollen clit. Without preamble, he grips it between his thumb and forefinger, rolling it between them.

I cry out as he rubs faster and faster, until I come with a cry and begin to fall as my knees won't hold me up anymore.

Nonno is fast: he catches me and turns me around, shoving his entire cock inside of me as he sits me on his lap.

I cry again, cursing, as my pussy keeps spasming from the orgasm, even while he begins to pump into me. I grip the cushions while he holds my hips and pistons into me. I've never been in this position before, and it causes his cock to hit my g-spot head on with each thrust.

In front of me, both Daddy and Uncle Tony have their cocks out and are masturbating as they watch my defilement. Neither of them look away from me at first, until Daddy stands up.

He walks around the chair to the side of Uncle Tony, still stroking himself. Without words, as if they've done this hundreds of times before, he grabs his twin by the back of the head and shoves his mouth down into his cock.

"Oh my God!" I shout, unable to contain my shock.

Both Daddy and Nonno laugh.

Nonno slows down then, leaving himself buried inside me as he says, "I taught my boys well when they were young. No cocks go unmilked in my house, even when there are no women around, or they're forbidden to touch them, like now."

My mind reels, though I recall thinking that before, recently. I just never thought it was for real. I thought my horny mind was away with the faeries.

He starts to move again, adding, "The younger you are, the more violently you are fucked. See how Eugene uses his little brother? We're going to use you even worse. We love you, but you're still just a low link on this food chain."

I moan at that thought and my pussy gives a few twitches. I come again, the final straw Nonno's cock driving into my g-spot while Daddy comes down Uncle Tony's throat, making him splutter and gag.

Uncle Tony's cock shoots jets of come into the air, and I feel Nonno empty his balls inside of me as I try to come down from my high.

Gently, Nonno moves me off of his cock, to recline slightly next to him. "Come clean your father, Eugene. Anthony, bring a warm paper towel and clean up our little one," he commands.

They both move immediately to do as he asks, and I watch as Daddy kneels down and begins to lick Nonno's softening dick clean of mine and his come.

Uncle Tony comes back and gently cleans off my sticky pussy and thighs, before he leans down and kisses me, tasting of Daddy's musk.

"Welcome to the family firm, tesoro. I think you're going to love it here."

Chapter Ten

Sasha

WITH SUMMER IN full swing, that meant I was at home still, and if I spent too much time away from home, Mom would think I was back with Trevor or hiding something from her.

Which, I am. Obviously.

I had to lie and say I was going to see the latest incarnation of Batman in theaters alone just to get to go to Uncle Tony's for dinner later this week.

But the week we've been apart allowed me to sit and think logically. I have quite a few questions for the three of them, and I hope asking them doesn't change what we have.

When I exit the Uber to his house, I can hear the music blasting from the street. I smile as I wait for someone to let me in.

That someone is Nonno, his large frame taking up most of the space in the doorway. He immediately pulls me to him in a warm hug and kisses my lips.

"Good evening, piccolina," he greets. "Can you convince my son that this is not date night music?"

I feign shock. "What? Nonno, Metallica suits *every* situation." With much persuasion, Daddy and Uncle Tony took me with them when I was ten to see Metallica, and I fully blame them for most of my taste in music. The rest I blame my mother and her love of 1980s new wave.

We head into the living room, where Daddy is playing DJ with the YouTube playlist on the gigantic flat screen TV and Uncle Tony moves about the kitchen, cooking and headbanging simultaneously.

I greet Daddy and then head to the kitchen, popping a piece of prosciutto in my mouth as Uncle Tony sets up an appetizer plate.

"Little thief," he comments, kissing my cheek.

"Can I help?" I ask.

"Nope. Grab something to drink, and we'll all hang out in a second. As soon as I check the chicken."

A few minutes later, I'm happily ensconced in Nonno's lap in an armchair, and Daddy is stretched across the sofa. Uncle Tony puts the appetizer plate down and sits in the other available chair, lowering the music a little.

"We've missed you, tesoro," he tells me, eating an olive.

"I've missed you guys, too," I admit. This is an excellent opening to the questions I've had, but now I'm nervous about hurting their feelings or something.

"Out with it, honey," Daddy comments. "I can tell you're bursting to ask something."

With a sigh, I nod and curl up even further into Nonno. "I have a few questions, actually. But I don't wanna start a fight or something.

Nonno pats my back. "Just speak. You're fine, no one's going to get mad at you for asking a question or six."

Remember they are nothing like Trevor. They won't tell you you're stupid or asking too much, I tell myself.

"All right... Well, I know we're going to see each other a lot once I start school, but I'd hate to go back to the dorms at night when I could be with you guys."

"Stay with us instead. I'll cancel the check for the dorm fees, and your mother will never know the difference, since you're so close by anyway," Daddy says simply.

"But..." I take a breath. "Where do I stay? You guys live apart. Do we make a schedule or something?"

Uncle Tony holds a hand up. "Wait, I've actually been thinking about this the last couple of days. Hear me out." He sits forward and points at Daddy, then Nonno. "Gene, you're still in that same apartment you took after you divorced Gina. Doesn't seem like you're in a hurry to buy a house or whatever anytime soon.

"Dad, that condo is nice, but let's face it: it's eight hundred thousand bucks for like, no space. I have a shit ton of space, and I want to share it with the people I love. We can all have our own bedrooms, and the fifth bedroom can be ours — all four. Where we'll be most of the time, but have the option to be alone."

His eyes sweep across us all, hope shining in them. "What do you say?"

"I'm all for it," Daddy says. "My downstairs neighbor keeps burning something in their microwave. No thank you."

I turn to look up at Nonno, who appears pensive.

"Hmm. I would like to bring some of my furniture," he comments slowly. "But I say yes, it's a wonderful idea. We can split the bills three ways and have more money for fun and spoiling our girl." He gives me a little squeeze.

"Four ways," I pipe up. "I'm gonna live here, too."

Uncle Tony shakes his head. "No bills for you until you're out of school completely. Whatever we pay you can be saved."

"But—"

"No," Daddy says roughly, cutting me off. "We love you. Let us take care of you."

As sweet as those words are, they bring me to my other concern, and one that makes me fear the response.

"What is this for you guys?" I blurt. "Is this where you see your future?

With me, even like twenty years down the line?"

"Yes," all three say, almost in the same breath.

Uncle Tony slides off the chair to kneel in front of me. "The moment I was inside of you, I knew you belonged to me. There's no going back, not for me, tesoro." He kisses me softly. "And once I showed these two the video, something changed. We've shared women in the past, I'll admit. But that was sexually, not emotionally."

Daddy picks up the narrative, "After I was with you, Tony and I realized we didn't want anyone else to have you, and yet neither of us was willing to give you up."

"So they came to me for advice," Nonno continues. "I began to love you just from their words as they talked to me. It was clear you were to belong to us all. You somehow wove a web of desire and love over us all, and we were willing victims.”

Finally, Uncle Tony says, “Eventually I know we’ll have to discuss marriage and kids if you want any, but that’s down the line. What we have, none of us want to give it up. Unless you want out, you’re stuck with us forever.”

“Forever sounds perfect,” I say, my voice barely audible. “I wouldn’t trade any of you for the world.”

“Does this make you poly?” Daddy asks me.

“Um, look around, man. It makes us *all* poly. I love you two just as much as I love Sasha, and I don’t give a fuck how wrong people think it is,” Uncle Tony declares.

"Hear hear," Nonno says. "We're not hurting anyone."

"'*Love looks not with the eyes, but with the mind, and therefore is winged cupid painted blind,*'" Daddy quotes.

I sigh in agreement, closing my eyes as I smile. This is perfection, and I will never let anyone ruin it.

* * *

For the next week, I don't see much of any of them. Nonno is busy moving furniture and selling his condo, and Daddy and Uncle Tony have both been questioned by the police for Erika's murder.

Good thing is, apparently Erika was sort of a whore. She had business cards for multiple men, not just Uncle

Tony. They're not putting much suspicion on him as her killer or the Northside Rapist.

At night, we have a group text which always leads to me sending them pictures or videos of me masturbating and using the dildo in my drawer. But it's not just the sexual aspect I'm enjoying.

All three actively care about me. We talk about our days, we joke, we discuss common interests. Nonno and I love black and white horror movies. Uncle Tony and I have the same taste in music. Daddy and I love the same books and TV shows. The age gaps don't mean anything to us emotionally. We're happy.

On Saturday morning, I get a text from Uncle Tony, "Come by at 7 tonight. We finished redoing the house!"

As I sit at my desk and try to figure out the lie I'm going to tell Mom, because I have a feeling I will not be awake enough to go back home, my phone rings. Tessa. I haven't talked to her since graduation day.

"Hello?"

"Hey, Sasha," she says, sounding overly bright.

She must be fucked up, I think. "Been a while. What's up?"

"I went on a weeklong vacation with my family," she said. "Now I'm wondering if I can take a gap year before college. But I miss you!"

The feeling is not mutual. "That's sweet."

"I wanna hang out! One last time before college. Please?" she begs.

I pause. I really don't want to waste my afternoon, but if I hang out with her and have proof, I may have my lie to tell Mom.

It's going to be wonderful when she thinks I'm at the dorms. Unlike a lot of parents, she didn't plan on dropping me off there. She said since I promised to be home once a month for dinner, she'd give Daddy the honor of dropping me off at college.

Daddy's still picking me up, but he's not letting me go.

"Sure, but I'm doing some packing, and then I have somewhere to be at 7. Can we meet at like 5?" I ask.

There's a pause on her end and I hear … something. Not sure what. Then she pipes up, "Sure! I'll text you the address, but tell the Uber to drop you off a block or so away. Hush hush little party house, you know?"

Oh, I know. If it's not one of her dad's clubs, those are the kinda places she loves to hang out at. "Yeah, sure. I get it. See you later." I hang up and then go tell my mother I'll be staying over at Tessa's tonight.

At 4:30, Tessa texts me the address, and I have to wonder what the fuck she's doing in Woodlawn. Her family is so racist, she wasn't allowed to go see *Black Panther* in the theaters with the rest of us. If this is her method of rebelling, it's laughable at best, but I bet her father would shit himself.

I text Uncle Tony and let him know I'll be with my friend and see him at 7 before getting the Uber. I don't bother with an overnight bag. I'll be naked when I sleep and can just suffer and wear these clothes again until I get back home.

The Uber lets me off a block from where the map on my phone tells me the house is, and I immediately feel stupid for not at least bringing mace. I'm in a neighborhood that has the most violence in Chicago.

I'm a fucking idiot.

It's easy to know which house I need to go into: Tessa is standing on the porch. But as I approach, the house's exterior and condition are alarming, to say the least. I think a gentle breeze would knock it over ... if roaches haven't already made it uninhabitable, that is. The stone is crumbling, and I think the porch has been home to a colony of termites for at least a decade.

Tessa, in her designer jeans and clean white top, looks totally out of place standing there.

There's a blue Honda four-door in the driveway, and it looks vaguely familiar. I assume I've seen it at school. It's not her car, that's for sure.

I wave, and she gives a small wave back. As I mount the steps, I can clearly tell something isn't right. Her eyes are red-rimmed and damp, and not from drugs. She's been crying. And her shirt isn't as clean as I thought, there's dirt and something light but unidentifiable on the front.

"Oh my God, Tess, are you okay?" I ask as I mount the stairs, careful not to step too hard in case the wood gives way.

Her arms are crossed tightly and she gasps out, "I'm really sorry, Sash. Please don't hate me! He made me."

"Hate you for what? Who made you do what?" I ask, confused. I walk closer to her and put my hands on her arms. This puts me right in front of the door, too close and too distracted to notice that it begins to open.

"I'm sorry!" she sobs as a fiery pain engulfs my right eye and cheek.

Chapter Eleven

Sasha

AS MY BRAIN tries to cope with the sudden knock to my head, I feel myself begin to grey out, not unconscious but definitely not all there. When I next become aware, I'm being dragged down a set of stone stairs. I can't see straight out of my injured eye, and the room is spinning. I'm still dizzy. The hit was hard enough to probably give me a concussion.

I'm thrown to the floor of a stone basement that looks like it's been set up to be a makeshift BDSM room, but nothing about this is safe, sane, or consensual. There's a wooden table with straps, and one wall has a rack with things like whips and cuffs.

One more punch to the same eye and any thoughts I have vanish in a wave of halting pain. Tears slip down, unbidden, and I just pray it's not blood, too. I want to fight back — I happen to be excellent at taekwondo and aced self-defense classes. But I can't, because I'm too damn dizzy from being hit in the head to try.

With effort, I'm lifted onto the table and strapped in, and as that happens I see who the mysterious "he" is.

"Damn it, Trevor, let me fucking go!" I cry, still unable to fully focus. I try to kick my free leg, but all that earns me is a punch to my gut before he secures it.

He stands back and admires me for a second. "Hello again, bitch. I told you you wouldn't stay away forever." He crosses his arms and smiles. It's probably the happiest I've seen him in a while.

"Sasha, I'm sorry!" Tessa cries from behind him. "He said it was me or you and then he threw me like a ragdoll and forced me to suck him. He said if I didn't agree—"

"That's enough!" he roars at her, turning to face her.

Fight or flight hits Tessa as she tries to run for the stairs. I could've told her it was foolish: Trevor is bigger and faster. He reaches her and grabs her by the hair at the foot of the stairs.

He turns around and faces me, holding Tessa by the throat. "I don't need you anymore, whore." He then meets my eyes. "This is because of you. If you hadn't left me, I wouldn't have needed to use her to get to you." With a move faster than I can follow, he snaps her neck, the sound so loud it echoes down here. Her lifeless green eyes stare at me as he drops her body to the floor like she's nothing. Like she's trash.

I scream in shock more than fear. He doesn't want to kill me, that I know. But my whole body begins to tremble anyway and I can still hear the sound her neck made in the back of my mind. If I live five more minutes or fifty more years, I'll never forget this. Ever.

Trevor steps over her body and walks up to me. He takes something from his pocket and I realize it's a knife. He loved using that thing. He never drew blood, but he knew it scared me, so that's why he used it.

Without a word, he begins to slice through my blouse, tearing it away from me. My bra follows, and cold air hits my sweat-soaked skin, giving me goosebumps. He doesn't speak, doesn't look at me.

When I'm naked, he takes the knife and runs it along my cheek, down my body, over each breast. It's an old game, and while it still scares me, I wonder if, perhaps, I can get out of this alive.

"Do you know how much I missed you?" he asks, voice low. The knife teases my curls. "How every night I longed to choke you unconscious while I split your filthy cunt in two?"

He moves back, pocketing the blade. I can't see him for a moment until he comes back with a horsehair whip.

He was never one for actual BDSM. I brought it up with him, because I figured due to his violent tendencies, it could help curb them. He read about the safe words and limits and colors and told me he'd never "restrict himself like that."

So what's the interest in whips and chains all of a sudden?

"You made a fool of me in front of all my friends. My family asked why I wasn't with you anymore. What was I supposed to tell them? They thought we'd get married!" he shouts, sending the whip right across my breasts.

I whimper at the shock of pain and reply, "Tell them you're a fucking psycho, that's what!"

That earns me another whip. And another. And a fourth one. I want to scream and cry, but I don't want to give him the satisfaction of seeing my tears.

"I love you," he insists. "And you are mine. No one else would have you anyway."

"You're wrong!" I snap, pleased to finally be able to tell him that. "There are men who love me — for real. Not your twisted, perverted love!"

He laughs, sounding truly unhinged. "Like you're uncle? Stupid cunt, that's not love. That's control, just like me. All you can get is a middle aged perv who probably wanted to fuck you when you were a little kid."

He whips me again, across my thighs this time. Tiny beads of blood appear on my skin like liquid rubies.

"I followed you after you left the party. Then I followed the guy who picked you up, and I remembered that house," he says, pacing now, hands behind his back. "I put two and two together after those two bitches on the news reported being abducted in the same area and then taken to your uncle's neighborhood.

"So I upped the ante."

"You killed Erika and that other girl, didn't you?" I ask, willing my voice to be strong.

He nods, grinning sadistically. "But first I made sure to get some use out of them. My dad taught me to use my product as much as possible to earn money. So before I strangled the fucking whores, I had some friends of my dad's come by and use them — for a price. Do you know what the chance to safely rape young, gorgeous girls is going for these days?"

"You're sick," I comment, and he punches me in the jaw. I can taste blood inside my mouth and I spit it as far at him as I can, even while my whole lower face aches.

"I wanted to get your uncle in trouble, but the cops are fucking stupid. So I had to use another ruse to get you to come back to me. And here you are." He cups my face, pressing hard on the spot where he just punched and I can't help pained tears that well in my eyes.

His eyes are wild but calculating. He's totally insane, but he's not crazy. He has a plan, and here, in an abandoned basement in a shitty neighborhood, I feel that he can get away with my murder, probably pin it on Uncle Tony.

"If you're going to kill me, why tell me all this?" I ask, in the hope to keep him talking.

Genuine surprise flashes across his handsome face as his eyebrows rise. "Kill you? No, you got that all wrong. I'm taking you with me. I have a villa already rented in the Maldives. My parents think you and I are going to elope there. And so will your mom once I have you call her. But that's for later." He grins again. "First, I need to finish your punishment. Then, you need to earn your plane ticket."

Before I can register what he said, he unfurls the whip once more and begins to lash my skin, over and over and over until my body almost doesn't register the pain. It's too intense for my brain to process.

Trevor's breaths come in rough pants by the time he tosses the whip away. He moves towards me again, but then a shrill sound of dueling guitars echoes in the basement: my phone is ringing.

Trevor stalks over to where he tossed my ruined clothes, looks at it, and drops it to the ground. The cracking of glass is loud as he steps on it, destroying it.

"Uncle Tony is trying to reach you," he taunts casually. "You think he'll be sad when he gets the news you ran away with me? Personally, I think he'll just move on to the next young, drunk, desperate cunt."

He kicks the phone and I want to cry more than ever. They must be so worried about me! Maybe they think I stood them up on purpose. Either way,

there's a new pit in my stomach as to
how much time has gone by so far.

Trevor hangs the whip back up
and walks back over to me with his
hands loose at his sides.

I close my eyes, relieved it must
now be over. And that's when he
punches me in the gut. I can't help the
surprised scream squeezed from my lips,
and he laughs as he keeps punching me.
I feel queasy, but nothing comes up.

After about a half dozen punches,
the beating stops. I try to catch my
breath, but it keeps coming out as sobs.

In the quiet basement, the sound
of Trevor's zipper coming undone is as
loud as a bomb. How did I not know this
was coming? Forcing me to have sex was
a regular occurance when we were
dating. He got off on my hating it.

Figures he gets off just as much on beating me.

He comes close and tilts the table so my pussy is perfectly lined up with his cock.

"Please don't do this," I whisper. "I'll go with you. Just don't hurt me anymore." Begging makes me want to vomit more than the punches to the stomach do. But if it gets me out of this, I can hate myself later. I just need to placate him, feed his delusions and fuel his fantasy. I did it for 4 years. I can do it again.

He strokes his hard cock, the head already purpling. Beating me must've been the highlight of his life so far. "Sorry, bitch, but you need a lesson drilled into you ... literally."

Bracing himself, he lines his cock up and shoves it inside me. I scream as he does; I'm not wet, not even from fear (you can get fear boners, too, look it up). I thank God he's not big, or else I'd be terrified of the damage he's doing.

I squeeze my eyes shut and move away and he slaps me across the face twice, irritating both my eye and jaw.

"Look at me while I fuck you, ungrateful cunt! Bitches like you are lucky I pay you the time of day!"

I look at him, trying to black out the feeling of his cock violating me over and over and over. His face is red and his pupils are blown wide as he smiles like the Devil. One hand comes around my throat and he goes to kiss me.

I try to turn my head again, but can't because he's holding my neck. His chapped lips find mine but instead of kissing I feel him nibble on my lower lip before he bites down and tears.

I scream as hot blood drips slowly from the wound, and then look up at him. My blood stains his lips and he licks it off and laughs. Both hands come around my throat then, and he pistons his hips faster, beating my cunt with his cock.

I pray he makes me pass out from choking me, but no. He removes one hand, and starts to viciously rub my clit. I'm wet now, but definitely not turned on. Not that he knows or cares about the difference.

"You're gonna come for me and prove that you're mine, got it? Or I'll make you join your fucking friend," he growls, biting my neck as he rubs my clit harder.

I sob as I come, hating him and myself and life in general. He finishes inside me with a series of grunts before pulling out and tucking himself back in.

Trevor slaps my aching pussy and laughs when my whole body twitches. "Good whore. I'll be right back."

He walks away, stepping over Tessa's body like she's a discarded Halloween decoration. I allow myself to cry more. No matter what, I'm not getting away from him, from this. No one knows where I am or how to find me, and by the time anyone reports me or Tessa missing, he'll have convinced my mom we ran away together. Death would be better than this. Death would be a welcome relief. But I've never been that lucky.

Tessa's phone rings, shrill in the silence as some new pop song blares. I'm too weak to struggle and even try to escape and answer it. When it goes silent, I close my eyes, trying to stave off the feeling of hopelessness that envelops me.

A few minutes pass, and I hear not one but two sets of footsteps overhead. Panic grips my chest, wondering what now? I find out soon enough as Trevor comes back into the room, leading a middle aged man in an expensive suit into the basement. He's short and pudgy and is in terrible need of a toupee.

He sees Tessa first and stops short.

Trevor looks down and waves a dismissive hand. "Don't worry about her. Collateral damage." He leads the man to me, and the man perks up when he sees me. "This is what you paid for." Trevor waves his arm like a model on a game show presenting the brand new car a contestant can win. "Eighteen years old, C-cup tits, bound and at your mercy."

"And no one knows she's here?" he asks him.

"Just me. Now, you have one hour. Do whatever you want to her, but don't do anything that will need a hospital … or a morgue. Got it? She's my property, and you'll owe me big time if I can't use her anymore," Trevor warns.

The man nods. "Yeah, don't worry. I'm not a killer. Thanks, Trev, I knew you'd grow up to be a real man." He fist bumps Trevor, who laughs.

"I've got shit to do. I'll be back when the hour is up," he tells him. He then turns to me. "I'd tell you to be good, bitch, but Pete likes you just as you are. Scream and cry and fight: it's only gonna make you worth the price."

He leaves then, and I stare at the man — Pete — as he begins to walk around me. He bends to inspect the table, and I hear a lever or something click. The table swings so I'm reclining back, almost upside down.

"There we go," he says.

I watch with a distorted view as he unzips his pants, revealing a thick and entirely unappealing cock, maybe seven inches? I try to wriggle, but that does nothing except make my breasts bounce and jiggle.

He laughs. "Open wide, rapetoy. I paid for all three holes, and I'm getting all three." He pries my aching jaw open, and when I scream from the pain, he cuts it short with his cock. In this position, his balls slap against the bridge of my nose, hurting my bruised eye. I can barely breathe as he slides down my throat. I want to cry, but that will ensure I suffocate, so I try to endure as he relentlessly rams my throat as far as he can.

He holds still, and my chest constricts as airflow gets completely cut between his cock and his balls. My body spasms in panic I can't control, and he laughs, rocking his pelvis to torment me further.

He finally pulls out and I gasp in great gulps of air. With a slam, he moves the table back the way it was, jolting my body.

"Look at those perfect tits. The whip marks are a nice touch. Do they hurt?" When I don't reply, he slaps me so hard my head bounces. "I said, do they hurt, you stupid fucking cow?"

"Yes," I say, and my voice trembles as I lose control and begin to cry slowly.

He grabs both tits in his hands and squeezes so hard, I'm half afraid they'll pop. His rough palms abrase the whip marks and I sob harder. "Yes, what?"

"Y-yes, sir," I say, hoping it's right and he'll stop.

He laughs and says, "Good fuckpig." Hands tighten again, and slip down as he pinches my nipples. Dipping his head, he bites them in turn. I buck my torso, trying to get him off, but it's like trying to get an octopus off of me.

"Fuck yeah. Fight me, cunt. Try and escape as I rape your next hole." He laughs and stuffs his cock inside of me all at once and I let out a scream as pain rips through me because of how thick he is. "Shut up, bitch!" He clamps one hand over my mouth to muffle the sounds as he thrusts, hard and erratic.

"That's it, bitch, you like it when I rip you open?" he pants. His cock pushes into me, stretching me. In and out, over and over. I'm not a person to him. I'm an animal to be put to use and beaten when I don't cooperate. He paid for me, and he's going to get every second of use. No matter how mentally scarred I'll be, he'll probably masturbate to the memory of my screams and struggles for months to come after this. And knowing I'll remember this forever will just get him off more. He doesn't even know my name, but I'll never forget him or how his cock raped me over and over again.

I moan under his hand, not from arousal but from pain. I squeeze my eyes shut and try and pretend I'm anywhere but here right now. Maybe if I dissociate hard enough my brain will permanently shut down.

I want Daddy and Uncle Tony and Nonno. I want them to hold me and tell me they love me and reassure me I'm safe. I want this all to be a nightmare.

"Tight fucking cunt," he continues. "I'm getting my money's worth with you." He reaches down and pinches my clit so hard, I'm afraid he might have drawn blood.

I scream beneath his hand, greying out even as I cry, my mind going blank.

Maybe if I'm lucky, he'll fuck me to death.

Chapter Twelve

Tony

"WHERE THE FUCK is she?" I practically growl, running a hand through my hair. For a moment, I worry I'm being too overprotective, until I notice Gene's face.

"She's never late. She hates tardiness," he mutters. "Text her again."

"That's text number five from me," I say. If there's nothing wrong, she'll be furious at us. I dial her number instead. It goes straight to voicemail. Sasha is eighteen, her phone is never far from her, and certainly never off.

"That was weird, right?" I ask to be sure I'm not paranoid.

"Very," Dad and Gene reply.

Dad gets his phone out and it goes straight to voicemail again.

"Think she's mad at us for checking in too much?" I ask hopefully. Because there are two other options here. Number one, she's deliberately ignoring us. Number two, something bad happened to her.

"Who gives a shit?" Dad comments. "This is wholly unusual behavior. Where did she say she was going?"

I check the text she sent me again.

"Going to hang out with my friend Tessa before we meet up. See you at 7!" It ends in a kissy face and a purple heart.

"Tessa. Is that the blonde girl she brought as a guest to my party a few years back?" I wonder.

Gene nods. "They've been friends since first grade. Let me call Tessa's parents. I defended her father in that wrongful termination suit in 2012. He's a prick, but we have a decent rapport." He takes out his phone, scrolls for a number, and then calls, putting it on speaker so we can all hear.

"Toole," a man's voice answers.

"Hey, Tom, it's Gene Santini," Gene says, trying to keep his voice normal. "I hate to bug ya, but my stepdaughter said she'd be meeting up with your daughter Tessa before coming to see me. She's now forty-five minutes late, and I can't reach her on her phone. Have you heard from Tessa?"

"No," Tom replies. "She left around five that she was going to hang out with some boy from school. Let me call her."

There are a few clicks and we hear a phone ring. He must have put this on a conference call. It just keeps ringing, no answer.

"They probably got a little fucked up and passed out. You know what kids are like," he says.

Gene's eyes flash with anger. "No, maybe that's what *your* kid is like, but Sasha doesn't do drugs, and she doesn't ignore phone calls from her b — family. If you hear from Tessa, let me know." He hangs up, slamming his hand on the table. "Fucking prick."

I leap from the table and begin to pace, wishing I hadn't quit smoking a few years back. I need a cigarette. I need a stiff drink. And I need to find my fucking woman. In my mind, I keep seeing that blue rental car picking her up and taking her somewhere to violate her before dumping her body downtown.

Bile rises in my throat and I swallow it back. I can't panic or think the worst. Not yet.

"Wait, was her phone just on before it went to voicemail?" Gene asks.

I nod. "Like she got the call and turned it off."

"Gimme a laptop," he says. I pass him mine since his is upstairs, and he starts typing. "We're still on the family plan, it's easier than breaking it up even after the divorce. Which means I can access her last location."

"I hate to be 'that guy,' but do we involve the police?" Dad wonders.

"No. They won't do anything. She's eighteen and hasn't been missing, technically, for even an hour yet," I reply. "Besides, if anyone has hurt her, we won't need the cops, we'll need the morgue."

Five excruciating minutes pass before Gene shouts, "Got it! It pinged off of someone else's hotspot at this ... what the fuck even is this place?" He pulls up the street view to show a ramshackle house that has seen better days.

One level, crumbling gray stone with a rotted porch that was once painted pink. The place looks abandoned.

"South Woodlawn? That is not exactly the best neighborhood." *Unless you want drugs,* I think. But let's be honest. Sasha and Tessa are rich Northsiders. There are better places to score drugs if that's what they wanted. Hell, Tessa's father is probably holding.

Whatever reason Sasha is there — or at least her phone is — it's not good. And nothing so simple as maybe wanting to get high.

"Let's go," Gene says, standing. "Let me get this on my phone in case she moves. Tell me you have something untraceable?"

I chuckle. "Of course I do. You never know. But if she's hurt, traceability doesn't matter. We're defending our family."

Dad nods. "Still, I'd rather not involve the police unless we have to. We're defense attorneys for a reason, boys. Now let's go."

I rush to my bedroom and unlock the secret base of the fake bench that sits before my bed. Inside of it are some ...

items. Just in case items. Items some grateful clients have gifted me after I won them their cases. Items I might not have registered with the state or city.

It's Chicago. Even legit people like my family and I have some underground connections. It's just how this shit goes.

I grab a Glock 9mm for me, a .45 Magnum for Gene, and a .40 Smith and Wesson for Dad. It takes me under two minutes to load them all and head back downstairs. After I distribute the guns, we head to my third car. I have an Escalade like my brother, plus a Ferrari, and I also have the car I used to use to pick up my victims ... um, former lovers. It's registered to someone who doesn't exist and who lives far from my address.

It is about 35 minutes give or take to get to Woodlawn from where I live, and I take mostly side streets and shortcuts to minimize any police seeing how fucking fast I'm going. I'm pretty sure I just took out a squirrel on that last turn.

I care about nothing but finding Sasha and making sure she's safe. She's my number one priority, and I know the other two feel the same. Anything and anyone else are inconsequential.

I park across the street from the house in question, noting that this neighborhood looks like it is trying to pick itself up. There are some abandoned houses, but people have small gardens and little window boxes of flowers.

Except this house. It looks even worse than it did online.

There's a man taking out the trash at the house next door, and Dad goes up to him.

"Excuse me?"

He jumps and takes us in; it's obvious we aren't from around here. "Help you?"

"Who owns this place?"

The man shrugs. "Nobody. But that white boy keeps bringing girls back here. Tonight he brought two. Guess business is good."

"Business?" Dad asks, just as I ask, "What white boy?"

He looks between us and says, "Pretty sure he sells drugs and rents the women. But I can't be sure. He's young, blond; gives me the creeps, man. And my brother was a Disciple. Drives a blue rental car. And that's all I know."

"Was one of the women tonight a pretty brunette with olive skin?" Gene asks.

The man nods. "Yeah. Didn't look happy to be here." With that, he turns around and hightails it back into his house.

"That has to be her fucking ex," I spit out. Blue car. That's the car that's been following me. I have no idea where it might be parked, but I can bet it's a bland Honda four-door from a local rental company.

"Is it bad I hope she's cheating on us?" Gene asks, face pale.

"Not bad," Dad replies. "All right, let's go in slowly and quietly. We don't want to alert anyone in case one or both girls aren't here voluntarily." He creeps towards the door, and I worry our weight is going to make the decrepit porch collapse.

"Unlocked," he whispers.

We step inside a rotted out living room. There's a kitchen and a hallway with four doors. Three bedrooms, one bathroom. Nodding at Gene, we move ahead, each taking a door and clearing each room, while Dad checks the bathroom and third bedroom.

Nothing.

"Is there a—"

Before I can finish my question, there's a scream from somewhere nearby, soft and echoing.

"Basement," Gene and I say at once.

The door to the basement is tucked away in a corner of the kitchen next to the refrigerator that must have been ancient in the 70s. It's not locked, but the door sticks to the jamb, and we all pause once I yank it open. Did they hear us? And if Trevor is down there with Sasha and Tessa against their wills, will he kill them if someone comes close?

We all scarcely dare to breathe as we hear muffled sobs, like someone's crying while their mouth is covered by a hand or cloth. Above the sobs is the distinct grunting sound of a man intent on destroying a woman's holes. Finally, rounding out the cacophony, is the sound of flesh on flesh, a rough, wet slapping sound that echoes off the stone basement.

"That's it, bitch, you like it when I rip you open?" a man pants. The voice sounds too old to be an eighteen-year-old boy, but I could be mistaken.

It's then that something shameful happens, as I hear words I've said to plenty of women over the years. My cock gives an interested twitch in my pants.

"Tight fucking cunt," he continues. "I'm getting my money's worth with you."

Gene clears his throat, and I don't need to look or feel to know he's trying to tamp down any sort of arousal as well. Dad is silent, but a quick look proves he's just as bad as we are.

We're men. And one thing all of us, except maybe asexual guys, enjoy is the sound of someone being sexually dominated. Even submissive guys get off on watching it or hearing it. It's natural for us, given to us with evolution along with things like opposable thumbs and the fight or flight response.

There comes a louder sound, like a muffled scream, and it snaps the three of us out of our lust-filled clouds. Fucking Hell, that could be Sasha! Ignoring the wave of guilt that hits me, I slowly begin a descent down the stairs, Gene and Dad hot on my heels. As I hit the bottom, I nearly blow our cover when I step on...

...A corpse.

It's not Sasha. This girl is blonde and pretty. Or, she would be if her head wasn't doing a one-eighty on her neck.

Must be Tessa Toole. Relief washes over me. Not that I want anyone to die, but it means the girl crying must be Sasha. Which means we can save her.

Dad puts his finger to his mouth for us to be quiet and quickly peeks around the corner into what must be the whole basement. He turns back and nods, his face pale with two high spots of color on his cheeks. I've never seen such a perfect mix of arousal and disgust on a person's face before.

I motion to my gun and then to the corner I need to turn around, and then to my eyes, as if to ask, "Can they see me?"

Dad shakes his head no.

Cocking my gun, I creep around the corpse, trying to ignore the noises coming from the man, and who is most likely Sasha. Something about a woman in distress is such a turn on.

Everything shatters inside me as I round that corner, however. It's not a random porn star in a carefully filmed video. It's my Sasha, the woman I love. She's bound to a wooden table used for BDSM and it's tilted so the pig on top of her can access whichever hole he wants.

He's wearing a suit that I'm surprised fits around his beer belly, is balding, and using my tesoro as a fucktoy.

I want to shoot him. My fingers itch to go pull the trigger, but I can't. If it goes through and through, it could hit Sasha. Time for some old fashioned action then. In three long strides, I get to the middle of the room, wrap my left fist around his collar, and yank back.

The man yells in surprise as he is pulled away, his cock making an obscene sound as it leaves Sasha's pussy. Before he can register what's happening, I punch him twice with the butt of my gun. The first one hits the nose, making blood gush down his face as if I turned on a faucet. The second is an uppercut that knocks him out cold.

"Come on!" I yell to Dad and Gene, who rush to help me. Dad goes along the back wall, where a rack filled with instruments of torture has been erected. He gets handcuffs and helps me roll the bastard over and cuff him.

Gene goes to Sasha, who's shouting and crying. I don't think she realizes who we are.

"No no no! No more! Get away, just get away or kill me!"

"Baby girl, it's us. It's Daddy. Stop crying, baby, I have to get you out of this thing," he soothes.

She stops screaming but keeps her eyes squeezed shut, even as Gene takes his pocketknife and cuts through the leather restraints. When she's loose, she tries to run but her legs give out. I rush over to catch her. As she struggles,

I hold her tight, trying to keep her from hurting herself or me.

"Tesoro," I whisper. "You're safe now. You're safe."

Her whole body goes stiff before she opens her eyes and looks up at me. I can now assess the damage done to her and want to vomit.

She has a black eye, busted lip, bruised jaw, and as I lean her away from me, I see bruises forming on her abdomen, as well as whip marks that are still open and raw on her breasts, stomach, and legs.

"Uncle Tony..." Her voice cracks. She turns her head and says, "Daddy... Nonno..."

"We're here," Gene says, taking his lightweight beige blazer and putting it over her shoulders.

Dad is busy getting more cuffs to use on the rapist's ankles.

"Why the fuck aren't we killing him?" I bark, holding Sasha to me as she begins to violently tremble.

"Because this isn't just about us. There's an innocent dead girl over there," Dad explains. "Honestly, did you forget everything you ever learned from law school? We have to call the police, or else they'll think we killed this girl, too."

Sasha sobs, burying her face in my chest. I shush her, caressing her sweat soaked hair. Her body is weak from shock, so I go to the furthest wall and sink down to sit, placing her in my lap. I wrap Gene's jacket tighter around her and tuck her head under my chin as she sobs.

Dad sits right on top of the rapist, ensuring he can't move when he wakes up, while Gene takes pictures of everything in the room to document it.

"Baby girl," he calls to Sasha. "Yes or no, did Trevor kill Tessa and kidnap you?"

"Y-yes."

"And who is this numbnuts?"

Sasha shrugs. "Dunno. I think he paid Trevor to ... to—" She bursts into tears again. "He — he threatened Tessa to make her trick me to get me here. And when we got down here, he snapped her neck right in front of me." More sobs; it feels like she's trying to burrow under my skin to be safe.

I hold her as tight as I can without hurting her wounds. If she needs safety, I will provide it. I will give her shelter and warmth and love and assurances that I will never, ever let anyone touch her again. Nor will Dad or Gene.

"Who beat you?" I ask.

"Trevor. He beat me and he raped me and I couldn't fight back because he hit me in the face. I got all fuzzy." Her breath hitches. "I'm sorry."

"You're *sorry*?" Dad cries in disbelief. "Piccolina, you were kidnapped! He knew what to do to incapacitate you. Don't you dare apologize!"

She tries to nod and winds up crying more.

Gene takes out his phone and calls the police, explaining everything as rationally as he can. "All right, police are on their way. We tell them everything except Trevor. His name stays out of it."

"Why?" Sasha asks, looking up at him.

"Because we want him to think you were too cowed to speak out against him. And then we're going to fucking destroy him."

"And the girl's body?" I ask, feeling Sasha shake against me.

Dad sighs. "Best bet is to hide her for now. Someone will track her phone and find her, but by then it hopefully won't be tied to tonight. If it is, it will go back to Trevor or this fuckwit over here."

I shield Sasha's eyes as Gene and Dad carry the body up the stairs. I realize what this looks like, but this is for Sasha as much as it's to allow us to go find Trevor. This way, she won't be dragged through a murder trial for her best friend.

"What if pig-nose over here tells them?" I ask when my dad and brother walk back into the basement.

Gene smirks. "You think he wants to add that he paid to rape our baby girl and let a murderer get away? Or possibly be implicated in said murder? Nah. He'll keep quiet. He has no choice in the matter. And if he talks, it will take a long enough time to convince the cops a rich man's son did this."

The man in question begins to rouse then, and at the sound, Sasha muffles a scream and hides her head in the crook of my neck.

Gene comes over and sits next to me. I maneuver Sasha so she's part in his lap, part in mine. We hold her tightly, calming her and assuring her she's safe now.

Meanwhile, Dad stands and kicks the rapist in his side. "Shut up, you brutto figlio di puttana bastardo! Che te pozzino ammazza!"

The confused man looks terrorized at being screamed at in another language while cuffed and sat on and then kicked. I grin, but there's no happiness in it. "Don't worry, Dad. When word gets out this guy pays to rape teenage girls, he'll be butchered all right: in the ass from his celly."

Sasha chuckles wetly, and the sound gives me hope that we really can heal her from this. It's not a pipe dream, and these bastards didn't break her forever.

"Please tell me we don't have to tell Mom," she mutters.

"Is your mother friends with Tessa's parents?" Gene asks.

She shakes her head. "She hates them."

"Then here's the story: the Uber you were in was in a car accident. I'm sure the cops are gonna make you go to the hospital. So I'll tell her for some reason they called me. You never saw Tessa today at all. Her death will be an unfortunate murder, but nothing involving you," he explains.

She nods and then bursts into tears. "I'm never getting over this. They fucking broke me."

"No," Dad says, coming over to join us while the bastard over there continues to struggle. He places a hand on Sasha's hair. "No, you're not broken. You're titanium, piccolina. Unbreakable."

Chapter Thirteen

Sasha

EVERYTHING AFTER MY men rescued me is a blur. I do recall the cops arriving, and I told them everything I told the men, except I left out Trevor. They were right, too: Pete didn't spill the beans either. It wouldn't have helped him, and he knew nothing about Trevor's previous murders, before Tessa.

Which reminded me, I never told Uncle Tony what he admitted.

The police wondered why and how the men found me. Which I wondered too. Imagine my surprise that Daddy still had me listed as a kid on the cell phone plan. I guess being a little taboo saved my life, in a way.

I had to go to the hospital, but I didn't have to take a rape kit or have a severely invasive procedure. Pete was caught red handed and then confessed. There won't even be a trial, according to what Daddy and Uncle Tony explained. Straight to sentencing: ten years for aggravated assault, kidnapping, and rape. He folded quicker than a beach towel, the cowardly bitch.

In the hospital now, my wounds are documented and treated, and I'm so ready to go home. I want to sleep for days, but I'm too afraid to do that here.

None of my men will leave my side, despite many nurses urging them to let me rest.

"I won't stay another second if you kick them out," I warn, and the nurse backs off. Daddy sits near my head, gently rubbing it. Uncle Tony is on my other side, holding my hand. Nonno is at the foot of the bed, warm hand on my ankle to assure me he's here and I'm here and I'm safe.

I'm so grateful.

"Here's what I'm going to do," Daddy says gently. "Make sure you're discharged, take you home to Uncle Tony's, and explain to your mother I took you there because it's closer to the hospital. All right?"

"She'll want to come by," I mutter.

"Of course." Uncle Tony caresses my hand. "And that's why I will put you in your Nonno's room. It looks kinda like a masculine guest room."

"Don't insult my taste," Nonno scolds.

I smile at them both. "I love you. All of you."

"We love you, too, tesoro," Uncle Tony assures me.

"Uncle Tony... Trevor admitted he's been stalking you via me. He killed that one girl and Balloon Girl." My head is so fuzzy, I forget Erika's name.

They all burst into laughter.

"*What*?" Daddy asks, and continues to giggle.

I groan and laugh a little with them. "That was what I called Erika in my head. Sorry, I'm a little fucked up right now."

Uncle Tony can't even talk for a few moments, while Nonno sits with his head in one hand, probably trying not to laugh. I didn't realize how silly that sounded until I said it out loud.

It seems incomprehensible that I could smile right now, but here I am, smiling. I guess ... I was used to the assault. Trevor never beat me before, but he'd forced himself on me more times than I can count. I know how it must sound, but I'd been subjected to a guy using me the way he wanted without a care, so it wasn't the rapes that hurt the most this time.

The beating is bad. I have a funny feeling I'll be flinching a lot for the foreseeable future, which I pray doesn't make my men feel bad. It's not their fault. At this point, my sister could toss a throw pillow at me and I think I'd wind up cowering in a corner.

But the worst part? Seeing Tessa's desperate, wide eyes as Trevor grabbed her, the horrified recognition as he began to bend her neck, and the same stare, now frozen in time forever, as she dropped bonelessly to the ground. I'll hear the whump sound of her body falling and the echoing snap of her neck in my nightmares and waking hours for some time to come.

You know in a lot of thrillers the main character gets stronger from her trauma? Yeah, I don't think that's going to be me. I mean, maybe in a long while, but not anytime soon.

My whole body begins to shiver as I sit here and ruminate, and I am quickly enveloped by men trying to keep my calm, trying to keep me warm, and trying to reassure me that the horror is over. But they don't understand. They *can't* understand that, for me, it's never truly going to be over.

Soon, a doctor comes in and says my scans are clear: no broken bones, but my ribs are still taped up because they were so bruised. Barring a concussion, I can go home.

"Is there anyone who will be staying with you to monitor you overnight?" the doctor asks. "Family, preferably?" He glanced doubtfully at the three men, obviously confused as to who they were to me.

Daddy raises a hand. "I'm her stepfather. I'll be with her."

The doctor nods. "Good. You're very lucky, Miss Santini. Most women don't make it out of that sort of situation alive."

Like he needs to remind me!

"All right, we're taking you home, installing you in my room, and then I have to call your mother," Daddy says as the three of them lead me to Uncle Tony's car. Nonno gets in the backseat with me, holding me tight as Uncle Tony drives carefully, like he's afraid I'll break if he goes over 25 miles per hour.

"Uncle Tony, no offense, but you drive like an old nonna," I mutter, leaning my head against Nonno's shoulder.

"Hey, be nice, tesoro," Uncle Tony says.

"Should I be offended too?" Nonno wonders.

"You're not old," I assure him.

Daddy shakes his head and pulls his phone out, putting it on speaker. He motions for all of us to be quiet as it rings.

"Gene? It's five in the fucking morning," Mom answers. "Is everything all right?"

"Yes," he assures her. "And I need you to stay calm and listen to me, okay?

I'm leaving the hospital with Sasha and—"

"*What*?" Mom screeches so loud it makes my achy head hurt more. "What do you mean?"

"Gina, be quiet," Daddy says sternly. "She's fine. She got into a car accident in the Uber she was in. She has a few bruises and a concussion."

"Why did they call you to get her? You're not even her father," Mom comments.

Thank God, I think.

"Both our numbers are on her emergency contact sheet. I guess they just got mine first," Daddy lies. "I'm taking her to Uncle Tony's to rest because he's super close to the urgent care center affiliated with the hospital. Just in case."

"I'll be over there immediately. Just need to make sure Maggie can watch Caleb." With that, she hangs up on him.

"Thank you guys for not telling her," I say as we pull up to Uncle Tony's house.

"I know it's the last thing you want, to be interrogated and accused the way she would," Daddy replies.

I gingerly step out of the car and Uncle Tony immediately sweeps me up in his arms, like he did that first night, when I was drunk and drugged. But this time it's different. This time it's out of love, not lust.

"I can walk," I remind him.

"Good for you," he replies, kissing me quickly, gentle so as not to aggravate the wound on my lip.

"Let's get you in bed," Nonno says, unlocking doors and leading Uncle Tony and I upstairs to the room that will be Nonno's. I know mine is done, but they can't put me there while Mom's coming over. Explaining it would be a nightmare and a half.

They tuck me in just in time; the sounds of Mom scolding Daddy waft upstairs, getting closer and closer. I feel my pulse race and anxiety spike. Something about the way she's always scolded all of us makes me react like I heard nails on a chalkboard. Because she goes on and on, usually tacking on things we did years ago. It's like a 7 layer dip, but instead of guacamole, beans, and sour cream, the layers are made up of our shortcomings and other various fuck ups.

Mom bursts into the room, and I can see worry in her eyes. "What on Earth happened? Were you driving? Tell me one of your stupid friends didn't let you drive!"

I bite my lip, agitating the wound. "You know I don't drive, Mom. And thanks, I'm glad you're so concerned about my wellbeing." I cross my arms tightly, feeling like a silly little twelve-year-old.

"Well, what happened? Why didn't you call me or have the hospital call me?" She mimics my stance.

"The Uber I was in was involved in a hit and run. The driver was hurt, too, and it wasn't his fault. It was the asshole in the blue Honda. The police are looking for it," I reply. "And the hospital called Daddy ... well, I'm not sure why. I guess he's on my emergency contact list still. I didn't call you because I needed my ribs taped up and my lip stitched and to be monitored for a fucking concussion. Which reminds me..." I sigh. "I lost my phone in the crash."

"I'll get you a new one," Daddy promises. He turns to Mom. "Gina, the girl's exhausted. Let her rest and stop with the third degree. The hospital said if there are no unexpected complications, she doesn't need to stay so near urgent care. I'll bring her home tomorrow morning."

Mom glares daggers into him, and Nonno cleanly interjects.

"Gina, carina, my son contacted you as soon as he could to ensure you were kept abreast. Clearly you cannot be angry with him, and certainly not with your daughter, who did absolutely nothing but survive a near death experience."

Nonno's voice is smooth like caramel, but his hazel eyes are hard. Accusation is clear in his undertone, and I watch my mom deflate. This is why he's the best lawyer: he's a smooth talker, and his veiled threats are like swift daggers. If Mom disagrees with him, she'll get to hear his real feelings, and nobody wants that.

Okay, wait, I want that.

Mom takes the hint and backs down, patting my foot under the blankets. "I'm glad you're okay, honey. And I'm sorry. You know how I get when I'm worried."

I just nod, not trusting myself to say anything. She turns to Daddy now.

"Make sure she's okay, Gene. I'll get some stuff she might need at home while she heals."

"Yes, ma'am," Daddy says. "She's got all three of us, she'll be fine tonight, and I will return her to you tomorrow."

She leaves and I sag against the plush pillows behind me, relieved. Originally, I wanted to see my room, but I'm so exhausted I can't think straight.

Uncle Tony sits next to me and kisses my forehead. "Sleep here, tesoro. I don't want to move you now. We'll have some food and stuff for you when you wake up."

When they leave, I do fall asleep, but it's not good. I keep having disjointed nightmares and flashbacks. Every twenty minutes according to the bedside clock, I wake with a start, afraid I'm still in that basement. And I promptly pass out again, only for the cycle to keep repeating.

The final time I wake, the clock says it's past 2pm and I'm screaming. The door to my room bursts open and I see all three of my men standing there. Relief and shame washes over me and I cry into my hands until Nonno takes me in his arms and lets me cry into his shoulder.

"It's okay, you're okay," Daddy says, sitting on my other side and rubbing my back.

"When will that stop?" I gasp.

"Maybe never," Uncle Tony admits. "We've had clients with trauma that never leaves, it just lessens. But I promise you, we're here for you. You don't have to go through this alone."

"Come on," Nonno says. "Let's get you washed up and get some food in you."

Feeling far too drained and shaky to even pretend I can do any of this on my own, I let them undress me while I hear water running somewhere else in the house. Daddy picks me up when my clothes have been discarded and carries me into Uncle Tony's bathroom, with its gigantic tub that has water jets.

It's been set up for me with a back pillow and epsom salts as well as lavender bubbles. All my favorite things, and things my ribs need to heal. As Daddy lowers me into the bubbles, Uncle Tony switches on a speaker with some of my favorite relaxing ballads.

As if I'm some sort of princess, I get waited on hand and foot. Honestly, it makes me a little uncomfortable because

I'm not used to it, but I am not about to
ask them to stop. It feels so nice as
Daddy washes my hair, Nonno massages
my bruised wrists and ankles, and Uncle
Tony gently uses a soft sponge to clean
everywhere else, being sure to be gentle
with my ribs.

When I get out, they surround me
as they gently pat me dry, giving me soft,
sweet kisses and whispers of their love.
Despite everything, one thing I can be
certain of is that my life is no longer
bound to pain and worry and threats.

I have love now, and that means
Trevor won't win the battle for my mind.

Chapter Fourteen

Sasha

AFTER UNCLE TONY gets some food into me, and I take a pain pill from the hospital, I feel exhausted again, so he asks where I'd like to sleep.

As much as I want to see my room, it won't really be mine until I move my stuff in for college. So I ask, "Can I sleep with you guys?"

Nonno lifts me to stand and kisses me. "Always, piccolina. I think we all need more rest after the past day."

I nod. I can't imagine the worry they were under, or how they felt seeing what happened to me. Picturing one or all of them injured and violated like that makes me want to vomit, and it's only imaginary. The real thing must be so much worse.

In bed, it's big enough for probably six people, but I still wonder how we're all going to sleep. They place me in the center, and then Nonno curls up on one side of me, while Uncle Tony cuddles my other side. Daddy in turn slips in behind Uncle Tony, using him as the little spoon. That kinda shows you how tall Daddy is, that Uncle Tony is the little spoon.

"If you have nightmares, we're right here," Uncle Tony assures me.

I nod. "Thank you guys for coming to my rescue. I love you so much."

This time, when I fall asleep, I don't dream. I know it won't be like that all the time, PTSD doesn't work that way, but I'm happy to have even one night that is nightmare free.

When I wake up, it's to whispered voices, and I turn to see Daddy and Uncle Tony trying to be still and quiet as Daddy jerks his brother off. My movements rouse Nonno, and I can feel a half hard cock pressing against my back.

"You got started without us," I playfully whine. I know it's super fucked up, what they all do, but they're not hurting anyone.

Uncle Tony reaches out and caresses my face. "Sorry, tesoro. We'll go to the other room, which I told Gene to do anyway."

Nonno chuckles. "Neither of you listen well."

"Don't go," I said. "I'm still hurting down there, but…"

"Go on," Nonno says, holding me close.

"I have two other holes," I mutter.

"And bruised ribs!" Daddy comments.

"I trust you guys to be gentle. Please, I… I want to erase what happened and replace it with the men I love." I look at all three of them, praying I don't have to beg any more than this.

Though Daddy still looks concerned, the three of them agree. Uncle Tony and Daddy get off the bed and Uncle Tony tosses Nonno a bottle of lube. Gentler than Daddy had been, Nonno slowly begins to ease me open, bent over the bed, and I can see Daddy behind him, jerking him off while his tongue is in Nonno's ass.

My breath catches at how utterly wrong it all is, but I don't have time to shame myself for being turned on before Uncle Tony presses the head of his cock between my lips. I give him a gentle suck as I look up, meeting his eyes. There's so much love in them, none of the hate and rage and madness I saw in the two monsters who had me.

This is what it feels like to be needed and desired, not wanted and used.

I suck harder just as Nonno pushes himself inside my ass, fitting perfectly, and I moan around Uncle Tony's cock.

"Fuck, do that again," he says, gently holding my head.

Nonno gives a jerk and I turn my eyes to see Daddy behind him, seated inside him as Nonno is within me. I can feel juices pooling between my legs, liquid heat turned on by the absolutely sinful nature of what's happening.

I use one hand to massage Uncle Tony's balls while I let the other roam over Nonno's toned upper body and he sucks on my breasts, careful to avoid the partially healed abrasions. I can feel it every time Daddy thrusts into Nonno, sending him deeper into *me*. It's like being fucked by proxy.

Uncle Tony comes first, shooting thick ropes down my throat as I keep sucking, draining every drop for him. His hand tightens in my hair, but he still doesn't push or hurt me.

Nonno stops moving for a moment and as he starts again, I see Daddy, kneel on the other side of my head from Uncle Tony, stroking himself.

Uncle Tony moves my head to the side and Daddy comes all over me. I open my mouth to catch as much as possible, but some still coats my cheek and chin.

Meanwhile, Nonno changes position, wrapping my legs around his waist and ensuring I don't move my injured ribs. As he does that, his cock drives deeper inside me. My whole body is filled with sensation, and Daddy uses his fingers to trace the semen on my face and makes me suck it off of them.

As that happens, Uncle Tony moves down, licking his father's cock, and going upwards until he reaches my swollen clit. Careful to avoid my still traumatized hole, he sucks my clit in his mouth. Nonno's thrusts become more erratic, and that combined with Uncle Tony's talented lips, I come with a cry.

Uncle Tony laps it up as Nonno calls my name and comes in my ass. It feels like he's flooding me and I lay there, twitching as I come down from my high.

Nonno moves, and Daddy and Uncle Tony take his place, cleaning my ass with their tongues. It's all too much and yet not enough and still utterly perfect.

I lay back and try to catch my breath when Uncle Tony moves me so that I'm laying on top of him, front to back. His arms close over my middle gently. The other two come and lay down at our sides, on either side, and I feel hot tears fill my eyes.

"I don't know where I'd be without you," I whisper.

"And we don't know where we'd be — besides miserable in our tired routines — without you, baby girl," Daddy assures me.

I love being right here, ensconced between these men. It amazes me that a little more than a month ago, I was in a quandary about Uncle Tony that one night, and somehow I'm here. I'm trying to connect the dots and I can't. All I know is this happened somehow, and I've never been happier.

I've lived through the worst things a person can, and I survived.

I was hurt and broken hearted, and I found love again.

And if I can do those things, I think I can do anything.

* * *

The hardest thing I ever went through … well, you know what it is already. The second hardest was when I got the call from Abby, my friend from school, that Tessa's decomposing body had been found in an abandoned house in Lawndale.

Her father reported her missing, but it was a squatter who found her when they went into the house to have a safe place to sleep away from the summer thunderstorms. It has been six weeks. Pretending to be shocked was so hard, and the funeral is going to be even harder.

Mostly because all of my men can't go with me. Only Daddy knew Tessa and her family well. It would've been weird for Nonno and Uncle Tony to come, too.

She was so decomposed already, between the time frame and the hot, humid weather, they couldn't have an open casket. But I'm glad for that. If I had to see her laying there, it would bring back how she looked when she died and … yeah. Not good.

At least I don't have to feign sadness as I cry into my hands during the service at St. Boniface Catholic Cemetery. Our old classmates are in tears as well, and no one can figure out what happened.

Some say she went to get high. Others say she was kidnapped. The police are looking into it, only because her family are such big shots. But I know they won't figure out the truth.

Which makes me even more determined to find Trevor.

Daddy, Nonno, and Uncle Tony have been searching, using every resource they have, but he's been a ghost since that day. Not even his family has seen him, but I bet they gave him money to run away in an offshore account. My men agree with me. But that means we may never catch him, and that thought makes my blood boil. He deserves to suffer for what he did to me, and die for what he did to Tessa.

After we all watch Tessa's coffin as it is interred in the family's section of the mausoleum, everyone reconvenes at the O'Connells' house for the traditional Catholic wake.

The house is, as I mentioned before, a mansion, surrounded by trees with a backyard big enough to be a park. It even has a pond. It is bigger than Uncle Tony's house, and yet there are so many mourners, it's packed wall to wall. Some are still crying, but in true Irish fashion, many are singing and telling happy tales of the deceased.

It is too loud, too happy, too crowded for me. I find Daddy talking to someone and let him know I'm going for a walk in the backyard in case he needs me.

As I walk along the edge of the property, I remember birthday parties held here, summer celebrations, general get-togethers. Tessa can never have any of those again. The only reason she died was because Trevor wanted me, and didn't need her anymore. A small part of me wonders if I'm at all at fault. If not for me, Trevor would've left her alone. If not for me, she'd be alive.

I know what my guys would say if I tell them my line of thinking, but I can't help but feel a little responsible. I'm the one with the martial arts training, and yet I couldn't save her. Hell, I couldn't save myself.

Sure, I got hit in the head. But something inside me keeps telling me I didn't fight hard enough, and I don't know how to turn that off. Perhaps I'll live with this guilt the rest of my life.

The thought is not appealing, to say the least.

Tessa never liked playing outside. She hated dirt. So while I was roughhousing with the boys and finding cool rocks and bugs in the copse of trees, she was running away from us before we made her get too close to a bug.

I smile to myself as I cross the treeline, wanting to be that little, unencumbered kid again.

College will begin next week, which means moving into Uncle Tony's house. Which is going to be awesome. Except it's another added lie of where I am, because I know people would all die if I explained my current romantic situation to them.

I just want to live and love and be left alone. Is that so hard?

As I walk, I hear rustling behind me and stop, fear creeping its cold fingers down my spine. I turn, but there is nothing there. The trees are sparse enough to let in the full moonlight, so I can see just fine.

I shake my head; it was probably a rabbit or even a deer. We have a ton of them here. Hell, there are even wolves. Taking a breath, I decide it's time to go back to the house and take a single step.

That's when I feel a hand in my hair, yanking me back.

"You're not getting away this time," Trevor growls in my ear. But this time, despite the pure fear within me, there is also a white-hot rage I didn't have the first time.

Without speaking, I whip my head back and connect with the delicate bones of his nose. There's a satisfying crunch and he lets out a strangled scream as he lets me go. I should run, but I don't. No running for me.

How fucking dare he come to the funeral party? How dare he piss on Tessa's memory by showing up here? He thinks he can have me? He thinks he can do what he does without consequences?

No. This ends here and now.

"You bitch!" he cries, blood leaking from his nostrils and staining his handsome face. He reaches for me and I bat his hand away. Using my elbow, I hit his injured nose again, and turn to run. Not to get away, but to get him closer to the house.

He grabs me by the hem of my dress but loses his grip. However, the movement sends me sprawling on my newly healed stomach, knocking the wind out of me. I can't get purchase on the ground to get up.

Trevor grabs my leg and starts to pull me deeper into the trees. I kick out with my free leg a few times, mimicking an angry horse. Third time's the charm, as I can feel my heel stick in something. There's a wet squelching sound and Trevor shrieks so loud, I'm sure they had to have heard it in the house.

I turn over, and my foot slips from the shoe. Horrified, I see where it got stuck: Trevor's right eye. The sharp black stiletto is impaled in there, and on his face is commingled blood and white goo.

No, not goo. That's his eyeball.

I want to be sick, to vomit and scream in horror. I can feel it all bubbling within me, but I can't indulge it yet. No, now while he's distracted is when I need to make my move, or I'm toast.

I dive forward and knock him back, as if I wanted to tackle-hug him. His head bounces off the forest floor and he yowls, using his fists to beat at my back and yank a chunk of hair out.

That's okay. It barely even registers. I have the advantage, and I won't let him distract me. Not this time.

I stare unblinking down at his enraged, clear blue eye and the other. The shoe fell out, leaving a grisly, gory sight to behold. He roars and keeps hitting me, but there's nothing he can do.

Grappling around, I put one hand on his throat and squeeze. He grabs that hand, distracted that I might strangle him. Good. That's what I want. With my right hand, I grip a jagged rock and slam it down over his good eye.

He screams and tries to grab me, but he can't see now. And I can't stop. I hit him over and over and over and over. Mimicking what his cock did to me, I do to his face with the rock. Skin breaks and blood splatters on my face.

I don't care.

He stops fighting.

I don't care.

His screams die out in the late summer breeze.

I don't care.

His body is completely limp.

And I still don't care. I keep pounding on him with the rock, even as my arm begins to burn with the strain.

I only slow when strong arms wrap around my middle and pull me up. The rock, now covered in sticky blood and flesh, falls from my hands and lands next to Trevor's lifeless body.

Not that anyone would recognize him by sight. His once handsome face is nothing but a mess of raw, bloody flesh. His nose is gristle, one eye swollen shut, the other melted onto his cheek. His lips are strips of flesh, and I spy a stray tooth in his bloodied blond hair.

"It's over, baby girl," Daddy whispers. "It's over. He's dead."

I turn in his arms and begin to sob from adrenaline, rage, fear, and disgust. And yet, his words ring true.

It's over.

Epilogue

Tony

One month later...

"ARE YOU SURE you want to do this, tesoro?" I ask as I unlock the doors to the Queen of Heaven Cemetery. It's past ten at night, but my buddy owed me a favor for getting him off a necrophilia charge, so I have a set of keys.

"I've never been more sure of anything in my whole life," Sasha replies.

Imagine mine and my dad's surprise when Gene called me from the funeral he and Sasha went to and said it turned into a murder scene. And then imagine how I felt when I discovered Sasha murdered that piezza di merda who kidnapped her and killed her friend.

I was so proud! Well, after I made sure she was all right. And except for a few bruises, she was. She didn't even need a hospital. Nor was there any sort of trial. Once I met with Trevor's family, the Doyles, and explained the proof Gene had that Trevor murdered a woman and raped and prostituted another, they agreed to call a truce.

Smart mother fuckers.

We were all pretty concerned Sasha would need therapy after what Gene explained she did to Trevor, but she seemed fine. In fact, her nightmares decreased rapidly after his death.

She moved in and started college, which she seems to love. There's a chance she can skip sophomore year and go straight to junior if she keeps up the way she has. I'm so fucking proud of my girl. We all are.

Nothing has changed between us. The living situation is working out just fine, though I know one day we'll have to tell people and face the music. But that probably won't need to happen until Sasha is out of school. Until then, we're happy where we are, living as we are.

Sasha has a three day weekend from school, and she intimated to us that there is something special she wants to do; a final form of closure, she called it. My dad laughed his ass off when she told us, and Gene and I were horrified. Honestly, I'm still a little weirded out. But what my tesoro wants, she gets.

Even if I plan on praying for our souls at Mass on Sunday.

"Baby, you know we'll do anything for you, but—"

"No buts!" Sasha interrupts Gene. "I need this. And I need to do it with all three of you." She turns her pretty brown eyes up at him and adds, "Please."

Fuck, she knows just what to do to keep us wrapped around her little finger, and we are all so pussy whipped we let her. Batting those gorgeous eyes would make us commit murder for her.

Gene sighs and kisses her. "All right, lead the way."

"You know," Dad pipes up as we walk through the darkened cemetery, "Mary Shelley, the woman who wrote

Frankenstein, lost her virginity on her mother's grave."

"Those are some serious mommy issues," I comment.

"She also kept her husband's mummified heart after he died," Sasha adds. "She was so cool. No one could ever measure up."

"Note to self: hide all knives when we get home," I say and Sasha laughs, the sound loud and joyful in this creepy place.

She stops walking and stares down at a specific grave. It's large and ostentatious, taking up multiple plots with its large marble facade.

Trevor James Doyle

2003-2021

Beloved son

"Should've added the words rapist and murderer on there," Sasha comments.

She turns to Dad and he nods, laying out the thick blanket we brought with us. It's late September, and the weather is cool but not so cold as to make our dicks shrink back like breakfast sausages.

The three of us glance at each other nervously, unsure of how to begin. I can assure you that's never happened before.

Sasha has no such trepidation. Immediately, she strips off her long-sleeved shirt, revealing a black lace push up bra. I see her naked or nearly so every night, and every night the sight still stirs my cock like it's the first time. She has no idea how truly screwed the three of us are, taken in by whatever spell she's weaved.

"If you guys don't warm me up, I'll have to admit you're bad boyfriends," she taunts. Her hands go to her jeans and she slips them down, taking them off carefully over her canvas shoes. "You don't have to get naked out here," she adds. "I only need your cocks."

"What happened to that shy, cute little thing I drugged?" I ask.

"She grew up and wound up living with three sex addicts," she replies, blowing me a kiss.

Dad is the first one to move, stepping towards her and kissing her hard on the lips. I can see his fingers leave marks on her ass cheeks.

When he pulls away, she laughs again. "That's exactly it. I want it hard, fast, and brutal. I want to show him what real men do to me." The look in her eyes is almost maniacal.

Gene and I come closer, undone by the look and by her words. I rip her from Dad's embrace and she crashes into me. I bite her lip, which has a small scar from the stitches, while Gene yanks her bra clasps open.

Those beautiful breasts tumble free, and any reservations I have about the endeavor are now erased. The animal inside me has woken thanks to her words. I want to claim her here, in the open air, on top of the grave of the man who wanted to ruin her.

Gene grabs her and gives her a light slap across the face, which makes her smile. "On your knees. Now."

She obeys, kneeling before the grave as the three of us get our cocks out. Fuck, there's nothing like a hot little mouth taking my cock down to the root on a cool autumn evening.

"Good little slut," Dad praises her as she licks his balls. "Get up, take your panties off.

She does as he says and he takes them from her. Walking up to the grave, he hangs them on the edge of it and then sinks to the ground.

I lift Sasha up and she yelps in shock. I then put her down right over Dad's straining cock, shoving her as far as possible without warning. Her scream is music to my ears. I grab her by the hair and slap her across the face.

"Open up, cunt."

She does so, and this time I'm not letting her set the pace as I shove my cock deep into her throat. I do it on purpose, because I see Gene getting behind her, and we didn't bring lube.

He lines up and pushes the head in. My cock muffles her cry as he seats himself inside of her. I pull it out to let her breathe and laugh at her face.

"You wanted it brutal, babycunt," Gene comments as he squeezes her breasts. "Don't ask for what you can't handle."

"She can handle it," Dad cuts in. "Her cunt is so soaked, I'm afraid I'll slip off."

After a few minutes, we take turns in other holes until we've all had a piece of each one. She's come three times already, and as she pants and cries as I thrust upwards into her soaked, abused cunt, I know I'm close.

It's Gene who comes first as he facefucks her, using her head as a masturbation tool. When he's done, her face is coated with cum she was unable to swallow and she moans in pain and pleasure and exhaustion.

"You love this, don't you? Being nothing but a three hole animal," I say, grinding my hips into her. I can feel Dad in her asshole, rearranging her guts. I pinch a nipple and twist. "Tell me you love it."

"I love it," she whimpers. "Only when it's you three." The last word trails off in another moan as Gene grabs her by the throat.

"Tell us what you are," he commands.

"Your — your fucktoy," Sasha stammers. "I belong to all of you, and you can do whatever you want to me because you're real men."

He slaps her again and releases her throat. "Good girl. Now, I'm gonna make you come one more time, or else we'll make this go on until the sun rises."

"Daddy, I can't," she whines.

"Yes, you can," I tell her. "Unless you want me to leave you here for the caretaker to find?" It's an empty threat, and she knows it. We're too possessive to even think like that. But her cunt clenches around me and I know I've got her where I want her.

I pump her a few more times before I empty myself deep inside of her. Quickly, I remove myself and Gene and I take turns pumping her cunt with our fingers and tormenting her swollen, abused clit as she moans incoherently.

Dad moves her so he can hit a new angle and she lets out a strangled yell. It's then that she comes, squirting all over the grave, even shooting out some of the come I left inside her.

Dad grunts and pulls out, cum now leaking from her stretched asshole. She flops onto her back, breathing hard, red-faced, tear-stained, but grinning from ear to ear.

"Come ... here," she gasps, and we obey, curling and cuddling around her as the night sky shines above us.

"Yours," she whispers. "My family. My loves. My masters."

"Ours," I reply, rasping into her ear. "Forever."

We're family, and family loves each other forever.

The End

About the author

S.L. Sinclair is a dark romance and taboo author fascinated with human sexuality, murder, and psychology. *Beyond Her Duties* was her first release, which made her an international bestseller. Followed by the surprise smash hit *The Family Firm*, cementing her in the dark and taboo genres of romance.

They're part of the LGBT+ community as bisexual and nonbinary and uses she/they pronouns.

When not writing, she's watching horror movies and has her nose buried in whatever book is closest. Sometimes she actually goes outside.

You can find them on Facebook,
Twitter, Goodreads, BookBub, and
Instagram.

www.ingramcontent.com/pod-product-compliance
Lightning Source LLC
Chambersburg PA
CBHW071448110726
47908CB00003B/555